THE
GREAT
SPAGHETTI
SHOWDOWN

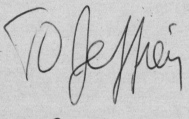

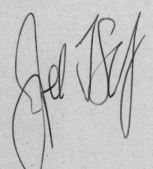

THE
GREAT
SPAGHETTI
SHOWDOWN

Joel L. Schwartz

A YEARLING BOOK

Published by
Dell Publishing
a division of
The Bantam Doubleday Dell Publishing Group, Inc.
666 Fifth Avenue
New York, New York 10103

The trademark Yearling ® is registered in the U.S. Patent and
Trademark Office.

ISBN: 0-440-40099-6

Printed in the United States of America

September 1988

10 9 8 7 6 5 4 3 2 1

CW

To Bob Clark, the Cinekyd staff, all the Cinekyds, and Sam the Wonder Dog
"Each one reached me."

CHAPTER
ONE

Skinny! I'm so skinny, sometimes I think I was really meant to be a piece of spaghetti. I once looked in an Italian cookbook to see if I could find a piece of pasta that matched my shape. The book said "the popular shapes vary in thickness of shell, diameter, and length." I figured I was too short to be spaghetti, not round enough to be macaroni, and not flat enough to be linguine. So I invented my own kind. Since my name is Eugene and I liked the "ini" ending better than the "oni" I guess I should be called Eugini.

When I was little I used to have this awful nightmare that it was raining marinara sauce and grated cheese and I was being chased up a steep hill by a knife and fork. I can laugh about that now but then it was pretty scary. I used to run into my parents' room and my father would calm me down and walk me back into my room. Things have changed a lot since then.

Six months ago my father walked out on my mother, and we haven't heard from him since. Mom got a job and we moved into a rented house. I now have the distinction of being the only kid in the world to be called "short stuff" in two different school districts during the same semester. Mom tries to encourage me by saying I'll grow, but I'm still a head shorter than most of the girls in my grade. The kids at school think I'm a wimp. It's no surprise I haven't made any friends at this new school. I didn't have any friends at my last school.

So what do I do? I've tied plastic bags filled with rocks to my feet and hung my legs over the end of the bed hoping that they would stretch. Unfortunately, the plastic bags always break and I have to pick up rock pieces from my shag rug. I've also tried taking triple doses of multivitamins. Not only did they taste like dead fish covered with marshmallows, I ended up losing three pounds.

Now I spend all my spare time in front of the TV and hope I'll get bigger soon. My mother doesn't think the TV set will help me grow or make friends. She's always trying to find ways to get me out of the house.

The other day I was sitting in my favorite chair watching the wrestling match between Crusher Martin and Baron von Baron. That's when Mom walked in and placed the newspaper in front of my face.

"Look at this," she said.

"Mom, can't you wait a second?" I said. "Crusher Martin is just about to apply the Atomic Crusher. Wait to you see what happens." She immediately turned the TV off and pointed to an area of the page she had circled. It was an advertisement:

HAVE YOU EVER WANTED TO BE A MOVIE STAR?
DID YOU EVER WISH YOU COULD BE IN A MOVIE?

LEARN ALL ABOUT MAKING VIDEO MOVIES
AT THE
CINEKYD VIDEO WORKSHOP
LABOR DAY WEEKEND
ages 12 to 16
for information call 555-4696 or
write CINEKYD
Box 469
164 Doowret Road
Uppermore, Pa. 19887

"Can't I become a movie star after the wrestling match is over?" I said, getting up to turn the TV back on.

Mom is pretty quick on her feet. With two steps she positioned herself between me and the set. "Aw, Mom, this is the most important match of the century!"

She folded her arms across her chest, the way she does when she means business, and said, "This is where you're going today!"

Every time she does this to me, I end up making a fool of myself. I decided she was not going to do it again. I folded my arms across my chest, mirroring her stance to show her I meant business too. We glared at each other. I was prepared to stand there all day if I had to.

As we drove over to this Cinesomething place, my arms were still folded, for I was definitely not going to go. "Do I have to go?" I asked my mother one last time, hoping to convince her to turn the car around before it was too late. "I had something important planned for this weekend." She kept driving. "I wasn't going to watch TV all day. I was . . . was going to call one of the kids from school and ask him to come over."

"You're going to like this place," she replied, ignoring my arguments.

"You never give me a chance to—"

"I spoke to the man that runs Cinekyd. His name is Roberts, and from the way he talks it sounds great. They teach kids from twelve to eighteen all aspects of video filmmaking."

"Mom, I'm not interested in making videos."

"They have state-of-the-art equipment."

"I don't care."

"Every summer they make a major motion picture and—"

Now it was my turn to interrupt. "Mom, when are you going to stop pushing me to do things. If you'd just let me alone . . ."

"You'll see. This place is different," she continued.

"That's what you said about the baseball league. Please! Mom, listen. I'll clean my room, and take out the trash twice a day, and do the dishes three times a day and wash the windows four times a day and . . ."

But she was determined. "I just know this place is different."

"How do you know? You've never been there." I hated to back my mother into a corner, but when you're desperate there are no holds barred.

"Oh, yes, I was," she replied. "I went there last week to check out the place. It's everything I told you, and more."

I unfolded my arms. I had lost the battle. I was going to videoland. "Do I have to go back again if I don't like it today?"

"I think we're here," she said. Ahead was a medium-size parking lot, busy with cars dropping off other kids around my age. Mom pulled the car into a spot and pointed to the first doorway of a two-story brick building. "If I remember correctly, the office is over there. Find out what time I should pick you up."

I slowly got out of the car and walked over to a door with CINEKYD ENTERPRISES, INC. written on it in black letters. Inside was a line of five kids and I took my place at the end. When I reached the front, a lady handed me a white pamphlet and said, "The door to the audion is over there. The program will be starting in a few minutes."

"How long will the program last?" I asked, wondering what the heck an audion was.

"It should be over by three-thirty," she replied as she handed the kid behind me a pamphlet.

Shaking my head and thinking that two and a half hours was an awful long time to be in a place I never wanted to be at in the first place, I returned to the car. "Pick me up at three-thirty."

"See you then," Mom said. She forced a smile in the hopes of getting me to respond. I didn't.

The audion, as they called it, was a small auditorium with seats for a few hundred people. There were still some empty seats in the first few rows, but I was happy to hide in the last row. I took the opportunity to look around while I waited for the program to start.

Black-and-white photographs of kids covered both side walls. Next to a projection booth in the back was a large bulletin board covered with weekly schedules. Just under the bulletin board was a poster advertising the movie *Return of the Space Monster,* to be shown "Friday, September 10, at 8:00 P.M." Now I was thoroughly confused. Mom said this was a place to make movies. The paper said it was a workshop about videos. According to the bulletin board, it was a movie theater. Where am I?

11

I felt someone staring. Beside me was an older kid with a tag pasted on his shirt reading CINEKYD STAFF. "Why don't you move up a few rows? It'll be easier to see the program."

"No, thanks," I replied, "I'm okay right where I am." As he left I heard some laughing, and it looked like a few kids in the first row were pointing at me. Silently I prayed for the lights to go out and the program to begin. I got my wish.

A screen descended from the ceiling. I slid down farther in my seat, welcoming the safety of the darkness. For the next twenty minutes we saw a movie about the history of Cinekyd made by the kids themselves. It wasn't that bad. The screen disappeared as mysteriously as it had appeared, and a tall, slender brown-haired man in slacks and a sport coat came out from behind the curtain. He took a pipe out of the top pocket of his jacket and lit it slowly. This must be the guy my mom talked to.

He cleared his throat twice and began. "Hello. I'm Clarke Roberts, the director here at Cinekyd. I'd like to welcome all of you to the Cinekyd Video Workshop. Over the next two days you're going to learn a lot about videos."

The first person Mr. Roberts introduced was the kid who wanted me to move my seat. He talked about making costumes and putting on makeup. When his talk was over, he divided the audience up into four small groups and showed us how to make ourselves up as clowns.

I was definitely not up for this, so when the kid next to me passed the whiteface, I passed it on. After all, people already laugh at me without makeup. Why make a bad thing worse? When the red greasepaint came, I passed that too.

"Just don't feel like doing that today?" I had no idea the voice was talking to me, so I ignored it. "If you're not going to make yourself up," the voice continued, "maybe you could help me." I probably would have ignored that, too, if I hadn't been tapped on the shoulder. Suddenly I was face-to-face with Clarke Roberts. He appeared much taller in person than he did onstage.

Still uncertain that I was the one he wanted, I asked, "Are you talking to me?"

Mr. Roberts motioned for me to follow him. Maybe if I told him I'd make myself up like the rest, he'd let me return to the group. We stopped when we got to a back corner of the audion. "What's your name?" he asked.

"Eugene," I answered softly so no one else could hear it. I hated that name. My father should have known how bad it was. It was his name too.

"Nice to meet you, Eugene. I'm Clarke Roberts." He extended his hand to shake. "The kids call me Mr. C or 'the Boss.'"

"I just didn't feel like putting on any makeup today." I looked into his eyes to see if he was mad. "I will, though, if you want me to."

"I just thought," he said, taking one of two cameras off from around his neck, "that if you didn't want to put makeup on, you might want to help me."

"Me?" There had to be a catch here someplace. "With what?"

Handing me the camera, he said, "I need someone to help me take pictures of the kids getting made up."

"Thanks anyway," I replied, shaking my head no. "I'm not very good at taking pictures."

"You can't miss with these cameras," said Clarke, still holding one out toward me. "They're fully automatic. All you do is look in here"—he pointed to the viewfinder—

"and press this button over here. It's that simple. If the light's not enough, the flash will go off automatically."

He placed the camera in my hand. "I'm going to take the group over there. Why don't you go back to yours and take pictures of them. I'll meet you back here at the end." He was off before I had a chance to give him the camera back. I stared at the camera for a while and then figured, What the heck. I'm as good at pushing buttons as the next guy. Why not?

I slowly walked back to my group and circled it, looking for a good picture to take. Out of the corner of my eye I saw the flash going off on Mr. Roberts's camera. He must have taken ten pictures before I finally had the courage to take my first. After that, however, I was snapping pictures all over the place until the workshop was over.

"Well, I guess it's time to go," I said, handing him the camera.

"Thanks for helping me, Gene. See you tomorrow?"

Tomorrow? I wasn't coming back tomorrow, but he didn't have to know that. "Sure, yeah, see you then," I said.

"There's no law that says you have to come back if you don't want to. I just thought you might be interested in coming here after the video workshop tomorrow. That's when I'm going to print up these pictures and I thought—"

"Thanks anyway," I replied, turning to go. "I don't know how to print pictures."

"Would you like to learn how?"

This guy was as persistent as my mom, but somehow I didn't mind as much. "I guess so . . ."

"See you at three forty-five." I nodded as he smiled and quickly disappeared up the steps at the back of the audion.

My mother's was the only car left in the parking lot

when I came out. I'd barely gotten into the front seat before she asked, "Well? How was it? Did you like it?"

"Slow down a minute, Mom. Slow down. The video workshop was boring." I saw her expression change from hope to disappointment. "But I had fun anyway. I met the head of the place. He's a really neat guy. I helped him take pictures and tomorrow I'm going back at . . . can you take me back here at three forty-five?"

My mother's face showed signs of relief as she nodded yes.

I rested my head on the seat behind me and closed my eyes. "What's for dinner?"

"I don't have anything planned yet. What would you like?"

"Spaghetti!"

CHAPTER
TWO

Around three the next day my mother dropped me off at Cinekyd and I went to Mr. Roberts's office. "You must be Eugene," said the secretary. "Mr. Roberts is expecting you. Go up those stairs. He'll be with you shortly."

Mr. Roberts's office was messier than my room. Papers were scattered over, under, and around his desk. Every inch of wall space was covered with awards and old movie posters. This guy was really impressive. I flopped down in a chair and was about to make myself comfortable when another boy appeared.

Although he looked about my age, we were opposites in every way. He was as tall as I was short, and pleasantly plump in places where only bones showed on me. There were no signs of a part in his short blond stubble, while my long black hair hung straight down, almost covering my eyes. His clothes were preppie while my jeans had patches on the patches.

Raising my hand in a half-mast wave, I said, "Hi, you new here too?"

He kept his hands in his pockets as he wandered around the office. "Are you kidding? I've been at Cinekyd for a couple of years now."

"Yesterday was my first time," I replied, staring at the floor.

"It's great here. Still photography's my favorite thing to do."

Maybe he's going to show me how to develop the pictures I took. "Is it hard to develop pictures?"

"Not for me it wasn't. I was developing film and printing pictures after half an hour my first time." I was right. He was definitely the teacher.

The familiar pipe smell made its way down the hall and into the office seconds before Mr. Roberts appeared. "Hi. Have you two had a chance to meet each other?" We nodded. "Since you guys are both new to Cinekyd, I'll give you a tour of the place first. Then we can go to the darkroom."

Been here a couple of years? I thought as I shook my head in disgust. This kid must really be weird.

The tour was great. I couldn't believe my eyes. Three studios for indoor filming, a makeup room filled with costumes and props, a special effects laboratory, a radio station, and tons and tons of all kinds of cameras, lights, microphones, video decks, and other equipment I had never seen before. The other kid seemed amazed, too, but we never spoke. He was too busy hiding from me on the other side of Mr. Roberts.

When we got to the darkroom, Mr. Roberts said, "Ready to learn some basics?" I nodded. "If you'd like to learn more about still photography or filmmaking, come here next Saturday and sign up for our fall programs. The kids your age meet here every Wednesday night."

Wednesday was an open night for me. As a matter of fact, so were Thursday and Friday and Saturday and—

"In the summer," continued Mr. Roberts, "we actually make a full-length feature film. Some of our past films have won first prize at the National Film Institute competition for high school and college films." He puffed his chest out and smiled.

"Long-distance phone call for you," said the secretary, sticking her head in the door.

"This will take some time," said Mr. Roberts. "Why don't you guys look around? We'll pick up where we left off next Wednesday."

The darkroom was a medium-size L-shaped room. Multicolored trays and an enlarger sat on a counter that extended the entire length of the long side of the *L*. A porcelain sink filled in the space at the bottom. Drying film and prints hung from ropes that crisscrossed above our heads.

As soon as I was sure Mr. Roberts was out of earshot, I faced the other kid, my hands on my hips. "What's with you?"

The boy stuffed his hands back into his pockets and rocked from side to side. I started to rock back and forth in the same rhythm to prevent myself from getting seasick. He remained silent.

I was much louder this time. "Well? Don't you have anything to say for yourself?"

"Could you stop rocking back and forth?" he asked. "It's making me seasick!"

"I'm making you seasick. You were the one who started rocking in the first place. Besides—"

The boy's face turned beet red. "I was?" He started to

gasp for breath, as if he had just run five miles, and he sounded like he was dying. "Listen, You won't tell Mr. Roberts that I lied about . . . you know . . . about being a regular here and knowing how . . . to do all that . . . photography stuff . . . will you?".

The kid looked seconds away from crying. I don't know if I felt sorry for him or just didn't want him to die and mess up my darkroom lesson, so I said "No, forget it." The gasping stopped and a broad smile slowly replaced the worried look. He took his right hand out of his pocket and shook mine for almost a minute. His palm was wet and cold. I couldn't wait for him to stop so I could dry off my hand.

"Thanks a lot, uh, I won't forget this, uh, what did you say your name was?" he asked.

Seeing how uncomfortable he was at this moment was like looking at myself in the mirror. "Eugene," I replied softly.

"Eugene," he repeated, and began to laugh out loud.

I save his life and this is how he treats me. Maybe I'll kill him myself. "And what's so funny about the name *Eugene*?"

Continuing to laugh, he replied, "Nothing's funny about the name Eugene. It's just that my name's Eugene too."

Now there was no doubt in my mind. Somewhere, there was a book to help parents pick names for their children, and it was divided into two sections: Winners' names and losers' names. *Bob . . . Bill . . . Eric . . . John,* they were surely in the winners' section. *Herbert . . . Arnold . . .* and *Myron* were in the losers' group, with *Eugene* number one on the list. "Isn't that name a real curse?" I asked.

"I thought I was the only one in the world stuck with it.

19

The kids at school are always making fun of it. They call me Huge Gene because I'm so big and fat."

"At least you don't get called Peewee."

Eugene leaned back a little to emphasize his stomach. "You think that's bad, how about *Tubby*?"

I got down on my knees. *"Shorty."*

Eugene puffed out his cheeks and as the air rushed out, mumbled, *"Tub-o-lard."*

I, in turn, crawled under the table. *"Shrimp."*

Eugene waddled over to me. *"Fatso."*

"Twerp."

"Porker."

"Midget."

"Look what the cat rolled in!"

"Still get into the movie for a children's price?"

"You're so fat, your rolls have—"

"Rolls," I said, chiming in with him, and we both began to laugh. I crawled out from under the table and looked up at Eugene. He reached down and we shook hands again.

"Think you'll come back Saturday to sign up for things?" asked Eugene on his way out the door.

"Maybe," I replied. "What about you?"

"I don't know. Maybe. I guess I will if you do."

"Meet you in the parking lot at ten, Tubby!"

"You're on, Shorty!"

CHAPTER
THREE

Eugene was chaining his black BMX racer to the rack when my mother pulled into the parking lot at Cinekyd. "That's the kid I was telling you about, Mom. The one with the funny name." I looked over to see if she laughed. She did. "I'll call you when I need a ride home."

I jumped out of the car and yelled to Eugene. I could tell he was glad to see me when I got to him. "What's up?"

He took a rag out of his pocket and began to polish the front fender of his bike. "Well, what do you think of it?"

I looked at it head-on and then walked around to the back. "The paint's chipped in four or five places. Are you sure this is new?" I asked.

Eugene looked concerned. "Where's it chipped? Show me!"

I couldn't keep a straight face. "Only kidding! Isn't this the new model with the special brakes and gears?"

He was smiling again. "I got it yesterday for my birthday. You should have seen my other one. It was falling apart."

I slapped him on the back. "Happy birthday. How old are you?"

"Thirteen."

"So what's it like to be a teenager?"

"My father told me I'm not allowed to go into the ladies' room anymore," replied Eugene.

"The last time I was in the ladies' room was when I was three. I was waiting for my mom and this fat lady, I mean big lady—"

"Hey, listen. It's okay for you to say 'fat' around me. No one else can, though."

"Shorty's okay too," I added. "Anyway, this fat lady went into one of those stalls and I bent down to look under. What did I know? I was only three. When she saw my little head staring up at her from under the door, she came charging out at me like a bull elephant and I ran like—I never went into the ladies' room again."

"You don't think I still go in the ladies' room, do you?"

"Until you just said that I wasn't really sure, but now . . ." I pummeled Eugene lightly on the arm thirteen times. "Happy birthday. Let's go in."

Just inside the door we were greeted by a brown-haired girl with a yellow badge on her sweater that read

CINEKYD STAFF
Hello My Name Is
CHERYL

She handed us each a packet of stuff and pointed toward an open room where we could see other kids sitting around a table filling out forms. We both stopped at the door to look for seats.

"What about those?" I asked. "Next to that blond girl?"

Eugene took two steps backward. "They look like they're taken."

"How can they be taken if they're empty?"

"My horoscope for today said, 'Don't sit in any empty chairs next to blond strangers."

"Are you coming or not?" Cautiously Eugene followed me around the table, but when we got to the empty pair of seats Eugene sped up and walked by them. "Where are you going?"

Eugene slowly came back and whispered, "She probably doesn't want us to sit there."

It was like hearing myself think out loud, but with one difference. When he said it, it really sounded dumb. "I have it on good authority that she hasn't bitten anyone for at least a year. I don't know about you, but I'm sitting here." I smiled at the girl just long enough to glance at her name tag, and sat down. Eugene sat down a moment later.

Inside the packet were two colored sheets to fill out and a schedule of the day's events. I glanced at the girl's name tag again just to be sure. ANDI. Probably short for Andrea. My hand automatically filled out the blue biographical information sheet, but my mind remained on Andi. Are her eyes blue or green? Is she a head taller too? What are her favorite sports? Does she like pizza with double cheese, mushrooms, and ground meat? Is she taller? Andi and Eugene. The two fit together perfectly. I had to look again. Quickly. Like I was reading something on the far wall. Like . . . but she was gone. I wondered if my horoscope said something like *Today you will meet a short blond girl who will fall madly in love with you. Play hard to get!*

23

"Finished yet?" asked Eugene.

"Not quite. I have to list my group choice on the yellow sheet and then I'll be done. What did you pick?"

"I've always wanted to be a famous star of the silver screen," said Eugene in his finest English accent, "so I'm putting down acting first. How about you?"

Big Eugene as a movie star? The thought made me smile. How does he expect to talk in front of a camera when he can't even ask a girl for a seat? "There's no way you'll ever get me to go in front of a camera. I'm sticking with still photography."

"What do we do next?"

"Next," said a tall, muscular guy in his mid-twenties who had just come up behind us. On his chest was a staff tag that said DAN. "You'll go in the audion to get your photo taken. After that you'll take a number and be called upstairs for a video interview with Mr. Roberts."

"A video interview? Do I have to?" I asked as I handed him my papers. Dan nodded.

"Come on," said Eugene. "It won't be that bad." Now he was the brave one. I followed Eugene to get our photo taken, and then we sat down in the front of the audion to watch others being interviewed while we waited for our turn.

"Are you as nervous as I am?" I asked. Instead of answering, Eugene took three long, deep breaths and stared straight ahead, his eyes fixed on the two large color monitors at the front. "I probably shouldn't be this nervous," I continued, as if he had answered my question. "You know, Eugene, you're probably right. It can't be that bad. After all, you're only on camera for two minutes." I tapped him on the shoulder. "Right?"

He continued to breathe deeply and stare at the

monitors. "Eugene. Are you all right?" He didn't move. I was beginning to think something was seriously wrong. "Do you feel sick?"

Then he spoke. "Eugene," he said in a monotone. "My name is Eugene."

"You don't look good," I said, feeling his forehead.

"I am twelve and three quarters, no, I am thirteen."

"Eugene?"

"I live at 340 Michner Street. I go to the Saint Francis Academy for boys. I like computers and riding my bike."

"What in the world are you talking about?"

Eugene suddenly came to life and smiled. "Well, how did I do?"

"Do? How did you do what?"

"I got myself into a trance and then practiced for the interview? How was I?"

"A trance?"

"Yeah. I got a book that taught me self-hypnosis to relax myself whenever I get nervous. It's easy. All you have to do is think of something good and pretend it's happening to you. Your whole body will relax. Try it. You'll see, it never fails."

"Number eighteen," a voice yelled out from the back.

Eugene stood up and started walking to the back, mumbling, "Number eighteen, that's me. Eugene. I am thirteen. I live at 340 Michner Street. I go to the Saint Francis . . ."

I was next. My heart felt as if it were going to leap out of my chest. On the screen I saw Eugene sit down and begin to talk. His idea for relaxation was worth a try. I closed my eyes and pictured the most amazing scene. . . . There I was, only much taller. I'd guess almost six feet three. A day and a half's growth of beard framed my square, protruding chin. I sat down in the chair across from Mr. Roberts and waited for him to begin the interview.

Mr. Roberts squirmed uncomfortably in his chair. Funny, he was the one who seemed nervous. "What's your name?" he asked.

"Eugene," I replied, taking almost ten seconds to say it. "Eugene Eastwood."

"Would you like me to tell you about Cinekyd, Eugene?"

I paused, and then in my most methodical voice replied, "Go ahead, make my day. . . ."

"Number nineteen, last call for number nineteen."

Eugene tapped me on the shoulder. "Aren't you number nineteen?" It was time for the real thing. "Hurry up or you'll miss your turn."

I went up one flight of stairs and into a room filled with cameras and hot lights. Behind a table out of camera range sat Mr. Roberts. He motioned for me to sit in a big brown easy chair.

"Relax," he said. "All I'm going to do is ask you some simple questions. Try and forget the cameras are here." He motioned to the camera with his hand and began. "New registrant number nineteen take one. . . . Hi, welcome to Cinekyd. What is your name?"

For a second the room didn't feel as hot as it had when I walked in. A second later, however, it became so hot I couldn't breathe. I opened the second button of my shirt, hoping to get more air, at the same time I started to say my name. My mouth opened but nothing came out. The lights seemed brighter and the room began to swirl. I grabbed the arms of the chair tightly to keep my balance. It was raining marinara sauce and grated cheese again just before everything went black.

The next thing I remember is someone putting a cold

cloth on my head. I was still in the brown chair but slumped over to one side.

"Is he all right?" I heard Mr. Roberts ask. "I think so," an unfamiliar voice replied. "He seems to have fainted."

I tried to prop myself up on my elbows but fell helplessly over. I felt like a limp noodle. What had happened to me was still a mystery. In a barely audible voice all I could say was, "My name is Eugini. I live at 830 Winding Road. I go to Interboro Middle School and I never want to be in front of a camera again!"

"Eugene?"

"Yes?" My eyes were focusing now. There was Mr. Roberts and beside him was Eugene.

"Are you all right?" asked Eugene.

I nodded. The cold cloth on my head felt good. I was even sitting a little straighter. "I'll be all right." I took a deep breath and tried to stand up. My legs were wobbly at first like a newborn colt, but they held my weight.

Mr. Roberts grabbed my arm gently for support. "Don't let what happened today get you down," he said. "It's happened to the best of us."

This experience was as bad as the time I ripped my jeans in school and all the girls could see my shorts. I got teased about that for the next three years. Can't Roberts see what I'm really like? "You mean you still want me to come back?"

Mr. Roberts chuckled. "Come back? You can't be serious. You have to come back to learn how to print and develop the pictures you shot last week." The room felt cool again and I smiled. I certainly wasn't going to be the one to argue with him over this. "In fact, if you and Eugene have time this Thursday, I can show you how after school."

"Thursday? After school?"

Roberts nodded.

"I'll be there. I'll be there!"

"I can be there too," said Eugene.

"Then we're on for Thursday," said Roberts.

Eugene put his arm around my shoulder and we walked out together. "One question," he said as we waited to get picked up. "What's this Eugini stuff?"

CHAPTER
FOUR

It was hard to sit still that first Wednesday night as I waited for things to begin. At 7:00 P.M. sharp, Mr. Roberts appeared, pipe in hand. "I'm glad to see some old familiar faces and some new ones too. How about if we go around the room and introduce ourselves? Let's start over here"— he pointed to a red-haired boy at the end of the front row —"with Tommy."

The boy waved to the group and took a sweeping bow. "Hi, Tommy." Everyone laughed. "I'm Lee," said the boy next to him. "I'm Colleen." "Stacy," "Tim," "Andi," "Wendy," "Aaron," "Becky," "Sara," "Amy" . . . There were thirty-two in all before they got to "Eugene" and then me.

"While the staff passes out the sheet with your group assignments I'm going to introduce them," continued Mr. Roberts. "That big muscular guy in the white-and-blue

T-shirt is Dan. Wave your hand, Dan. He's in charge of the technical crew. The skinny guy with the long hair and mustache is Marc and just behind him in the Seattle Seahawks cap is Eric. They both help me with TV talent. On the other side of the audion in the jeans is Peggy. She's with makeup and costumes. Behind her, wearing the denim skirt, is Paula of still photography. Over by the wall wearing the white shirt is 'Mr. Fixit,' Ralph. And last, but not least, is Jon, the head of mobile video. When you find out what group you're in, go to your group leader and he or she will take you to where you'll be going to meet. Any questions? Good, we'll all meet back here for the wrap-up at nine."

Eugene jumped up almost before Mr. Roberts finished, and headed for the front of the audion. I stood around in the row and watched everyone go.

"Hi." There at the end of the row was the blond girl I'd sat next to when I signed up.

"Hi." My throat felt dry and I had a difficult time swallowing. She was really good-looking and she was talking to me.

"What group are you in?"

She definitely had blue eyes and red lips and two ears and . . . "Hi."

"Hi again. What group are you in?"

The best thing of all was, we were both the same size. "I think I'm taller than you."

The girl shook her head and looked at me as if I were from Mars. "What does that have to do with what group you're in?"

"What does what have to do with what?" I asked as I began to rock back and forth.

"Let's begin again," she said. "Hi."

"Hi." I smiled, knowing that I had given the right answer this time.

"What group are you in?"

"Still photography." I was really cooking. Two right answers in a row. "What are you in?" Followed by the right question. My rocking stopped.

"TV tech. You know, working the cameras, the lighting, the sound."

Later on I thought of a million things I could have said next, but then all that came out was an "Oh," some silence, and then a clever "I've got to go to my group now."

The girl waved. "See ya around." And left for her group. I bumped into the last three chairs as I backed out of my row. Having difficulty walking and staring at the same time? I asked myself.

I was replaying my meeting with Andi when the head of still photography came over. "Hi, I'm Paula. Ready to go upstairs?"

"Huh? Where do we go?"

"Upstairs to the darkroom."

I looked around. There was no one else in my group. "Didn't anybody else pick this?" I asked as I followed her upstairs.

"Most of the kids pick acting," said Paula. "Me, I prefer to be on the other side of the camera." I'll second that, I thought. Somehow for now that seemed safer. "This is your first year here, isn't it?" I nodded. "This is my fifth. I started here when I was twelve."

"How long's this place been around?" I asked.

"Ten years," replied Paula. "It started in Mr. Roberts's basement."

"In his basement?"

"Five kids, some lights, and a super-eight movie camera.

31

That year the kids made a movie about Cinekyd. Mr. Roberts used that movie when he went into the community to raise money. His fund-raising campaign was so successful that he was able to move the operation from his basement to a vacant bus garage and buy some more equipment. The next year more kids came, the program was a little better, and more money was raised. We moved into this place two years later."

"What does Mr. Roberts do during the day?"

"During the week he's head of media services at the high school across town. He's here every day after school and all weekend."

"When does he get time to spend with his family?" I asked.

"He's divorced," said Paula.

"Divorced?" I repeated loudly.

"For about seven years now," said Paula.

He didn't look like he was divorced. Dumb, thought Eugene. How does a person look who's divorced?

"We'd better get to work."

I nodded, but that's not what I was thinking about. I wondered if my parents would eventually get divorced. Funny, I wasn't even sure if they were officially separated.

"I want you to take pictures of the TV talent group." I guess I never asked Mom about it because I didn't want to hear something bad. "That group is usually divided in half, so shoot the half that's in the audion tonight and next week you can do the other half that's in studio one." Paula pointed to a black leather case on the table. "Take that camera over there."

I got the camera and started for the door. "Studio one?"

"No, the audion," she repeated.

I quickly made my way downstairs to the audion but

stood in the back corner for a long time just watching and listening and thinking.

"You need more than just words to create a character on the screen," said Mr. Roberts as he walked back and forth, arms flying in all directions, in front of the kids in this group.

I crept closer and focused my camera on his face and waited. Why had he gotten divorced? Where was the rest of his family? Did he have any kids?

"You have to show emotions with your face, like this . . ." This was a good picture to start with. *Click* ". . . your body . . ." *Click* ". . . your gestures . . ." *Click* "Tonight we're going to concentrate on making every part of your face come alive. Now everyone think of an emotion. When I call you up I want you to portray that emotion using only your facial expressions. Then we'll try to guess it. Okay, Lee, you're first."

What had my face shown Paula when she said, "He's divorced"? Surprise? Frustration? Sadness? Anger? Coolness? Nothing? Everything?

I shot pictures through a mental fog that night. Four rolls in all. At nine I was back in the audion next to Eugene.

"What'd you do tonight?" I asked.

"I was picked to be the lead in the Cinekyd weekly serial and I spent my whole evening learning seven pages of dialogue. What did you do?"

He was lying again, but why? "I took over a thousand pictures of the kids in the audion," I replied smugly.

"There wasn't enough time to take a thousand pictures," he replied.

"If there was time enough to learn seven pages of script, there had to be time to shoot a thousand pictures."

Eugene's face turned bright red. "I had one line of dia-

33

logue to learn and every time we went to shoot the scene, I forgot it. I was awful tonight."

"Don't worry about it. My pictures probably weren't any good tonight either. So what? There's always next week."

"Yeah," replied Eugene. "Next time."

I laughed to myself about that on the ride home. Something historic had just happened. The world's most pessimistic person had just told someone not to worry and be optimistic. I made a mental note of the day and time. Maybe there was some hope for me too.

CHAPTER
FIVE

As great as things were at Cinekyd, that's how bad they
were at school. To survive, I walked briskly between classes
with my whole body scrunched over and my head down,
hoping to get lost in the crowd.

I was on the way to my locker after school one autumn
day to get my books when it started.

"Gene? It is you!" I turned around and there standing
beside me was the blond girl from Cinekyd. Her eyes shone
and her head bobbed from side to side as she continued. "I
thought I heard somebody at Cinekyd say you went to this
school, but I never saw you around."

"Hi . . ." Her name was on the tip of my tongue. I knew
it ended in an *i* . . . Was it Terri? no . . . Mindi? no . . .
Mandi, Debbi, Judi? no . . . Lori, Staci, Traci, Candi,
Randi, Sandi . . . "Andi! Hi, Andi! I'm here all right. We
moved here last May." I took three deep breaths, pulled my

pants up, pushed my hair out of my eyes, and smiled. This was my chance to make an impression on the only girl in the world who's shorter than me and is willing to talk to me. "So . . . um . . . aaah . . . So, hi."

Andi took a step closer. "What do you think of the school?"

"It's okay, I guess. I mean, it's not that bad really. It's sort of good sometimes too." I put my hands in my pockets, took them out, folded my arms, unfolded my arms, and hid my hands behind my back.

"Who are your teachers?"

"Let's see . . . For English I have—"

"Hey, Shorty!"

"Mr. Johnson."

"Hey, Shorty! Don't you answer when somebody talks to you?"

Andi shook her head in disgust. "Do you know that jerk?"

I glanced over my shoulder. A boy, slightly taller than me but with huge massive gigantic impressive muscular arms, was marching toward me. I had two choices. To get out of there as quickly as I could, or to get out of there quicker than that. I choose the latter. "Listen, I have to go. My mother's picking me up after school today so I can get a new pair of sneakers." Andi looked down at the sneakers I was wearing just as I remembered they were almost new. Too embarrassed to look her straight in the eye and too scared to stay much longer, I took off down the hall. "I'm going to get another pair just like these, only a half size bigger. You know how fast feet grow at this age. See ya."

Halfway down that hall, I heard pounding feet followed by the ominous *"Hey, Shorty! Get over here now!"* Petrified, I stopped dead in my tracks and then started toward the sneering boy and his two buddies. "That's a good Shorty. There's no need to run. I just wanted to say hello and welcome you to our school. We usually don't wait until November to do this, but somehow you slipped by the welcoming committee."

I forced a small smile and started to rock. "Move and you're dead!" If I made it out of there alive, I'd have to face Andi again, so maybe death was a good compromise.

"Hey, Todd!" yelled another kid from down the hall. "Is our match at home or away tomorrow?" That was just the distraction I needed. When Todd turned to answer, my rocking changed to running and I took off.

"Get back here, you wimp!" I had too much of a head start on them this time to be caught. "Just wait. The school ain't that big. You'll get your greeting another day."

I ran right by my math room and didn't stop until I got to the front of the school. I'd be safe there until my mother came to take me to Cinekyd. This replaced the undershorts episode as number one. I sat down on the sidewalk to catch my breath. What else could I have done? Stay there and fight? What's better, a dead hero or a live wimp? Probably neither.

An old red Mustang pulled into the driveway and, to my alarm, stopped right in front of where I was standing. The driver waved and beeped the horn. I pretended not to notice. Finally the window rolled down and a voice hollered, "Eugene! Is that you?" My first impulse was to run again, but I stood my ground and shaded my eyes with my hand, hoping to make out who was calling me. "Eugene?" the voice repeated, uncertain now of his first impression. "Is that you?"

It wasn't until I took a step forward and the driver stuck his head out the window that I realized it was Dan. "Oh,

Dan, hi. I didn't recognize you at first. What are you doing here?"

Dan smiled. "I'm the J.V. wrestling coach. The season started last week. Listen, I'm running late as usual. I gotta go. See you at Cinekyd."

It wasn't too much after that, that my mother arrived. Even though I looked calm outwardly, inside was a different story. In my mind I was simultaneously beating Todd up for picking on me and beating myself up for being such a wimp. Next time I'll beat the crap out of that guy, I told myself. Wasn't this the next time from last time? The comfort of Cinekyd was not far away. I looked forward to seeing Mr. Roberts. I'd never met anyone like him before. He was the greatest.

But today even he seemed to turn against me. Tacked to the bulletin board in the darkroom was a piece of paper with my name on it. Inside were five pictures I had done last week, with the following message.

> *These prints are not very good.*
> *Could you please do them over?*
> *Thanks.*
> *The Boss*

I held the pictures up to the light and shook my head. "What's the matter with these pictures?" I mumbled out loud, tossing them onto the counter beside the developing trays. "Nothing's the matter, that's what's the matter." I kicked the stool beside me and sent it crashing to the floor. "This is just what I need today, another person to give me grief. Well, Mr. Roberts," I proclaimed, "I'm doing the pictures I want today and if you don't like it"—I lowered my voice a little, just in case—"that's tough."

38

When today's pictures were ready, I put them in a pile on the table. I spread the five pictures from last week out in front of me. Maybe they could use a little more contrast or be a little sharper. I scooped them up with my hand and put them under the finished pictures. No one else was going to push me around today.

On my way down to Mr. Roberts's office I smiled to myself, thinking, He'll never know. I waited at the door while he finished a phone call.

I cleared my throat to announce my presence. "Here are the press pictures." Without changing his expression, Mr. Roberts snatched them out of my hand and rapidly looked through them. When he came to the ones from last week, he stopped and lined them up side by side in front of him on the desk.

"I'll see you next Wednesday night," I said as I backed quietly out of the room.

I hadn't gotten quite to the door when he looked up. "Wait a minute, young man!" I froze. "These prints are still terrible!"

I took a deep breath and swallowed before meekly asking, "What's the matter with them?"

"This one," he replied, pointing to the first one, "is too light. These," pointing to the second and third, "are too dark, and the focus in the last two is poor." He scooped up the pictures in one hand and tossed them toward me, saying, "I think you should do them over again."

I wasn't expecting them to be thrown back at me. As they hit my outstretched hand they scattered all over the floor. I stared at Mr. Roberts. With trembling hands I gathered up the pictures and left. On the way to the darkroom I crumpled them up in one hand and flung them full force against the back wall as I walked in. Then I headed for the

39

front door. Fast! Then I felt sad. It was hard to see the man I admired act like such a jerk.

When I got to the edge of the parking lot, I turned, and in a louder than normal voice, yelled, "Who do you think you are anyway, *Mr. Bossman Roberts*? Just because my pictures aren't up to *your* standards doesn't give you the right to throw them at me. My father never threw anything at me. You could pay me a million dollars, no, a zillion dollars, to come back here. I won't. *W . . . O . . . N . . . T.* Won't!"

CHAPTER
SIX

An hour later I stomped into the house. Mom was pacing back and forth in the kitchen. "Where have you been? Is everything okay?"

What went on at Cinekyd between Mr. Roberts and me was private. "I'm fine."

"I thought you were going to call me when you needed a ride home."

"I got done early. It was a nice day so I decided to walk home. I'll be in my room doing my homework if you need me."

When I was halfway up the stairs, my mother said, "By the way, Mr. Roberts called you." I turned around and walked back into the kitchen. "Twice."

It was important not to look too interested. "What did he want?"

"All he said was, tell Eugene to call me when he gets home."

...ce, I thought. "I'll call him later," I replied as I ...pstairs again. "I have a lot of homework to do."

Call him, sure I'll call him. What does he think I am, stupid or something? I settled in at my desk and started reading my history book. Fifteen minutes later, still on the same page, I slammed the book closed. "Who does that guy think he is anyway? He has no right telling me what to do."

I gritted my teeth and made faces at the wall. My fist landed squarely on the cardboard pencil cup I made in second grade, sending the pencils inside it flying. "If there was just some way I could get back at you, I would. Boss, huh? Not boss over me!"

I picked up my book and tried to read again. It was no use. If I could find something that would say to him *"IN YOUR FACE, MR. ROBERTS."* Something that . . . I paused because it had just occurred to me how I could do it.

I went downstairs and put on my coat. "I left something important at Cinekyd and I have to bike over and get it." I was sure Mom would protest over such a bogus excuse. "I also forgot to do one of my jobs, so I might be there a little while." Again I waited for the objection. "Save a little dinner for me."

As I headed for the garage Mom patted me on the shoulder and said, "Be careful biking over." I searched her face. She had known all along.

When I arrived at Cinekyd, I went directly to the darkroom. The negatives for the pictures that had to be redone were still hanging up. I made several prints of each picture, paying more attention to time and temperature than I would have normally. With the best of each print in hand I marched down the hall to Mr. Roberts's office.

The Boss was sitting at his desk reading something.

Without saying a word I tossed the pictures in front of him and started to leave.

"These are the best prints you've ever done," he said. I continued to walk. "A professional couldn't have done— Hey, where are you going?"

My eyes widened as I turned and yelled, "I'm going home. This is my last day here! I quit!"

"Quit?" said Mr. Roberts, mystified. He walked around to the front of the desk, as if to follow after me, and repeated, "Quit?"

I did nothing to hide the fact I was angry. "Why did you throw those pictures at me today?"

"Throw the pictures at you? I wasn't throwing them at you, I was just tossing them to you."

I couldn't believe I said what I said next. "No, you didn't. You threw them at me and *YOU KNOW IT!*"

For a minute Mr. Roberts was stone silent, and I wondered what he was thinking. Anything I came up with wasn't good. Maybe I should apologize. When he finally spoke, he sounded a little angry and a little apologetic. "I only meant to toss the pictures to you, but maybe I did throw them. You did get me a little mad."

"Mad?" Had he known I hadn't really done them over? "What were you mad about?"

"Your prints," said Mr. Roberts, resting his right hand on my shoulder, "were as bad as the originals." He removed his hand and pointed his index finger straight at me. "But that isn't really what got to me, though. What really made me mad was that you were satisfied with them." Mr. Roberts put his hand back on my shoulder and gave it a squeeze. "Maybe I didn't do it the right way, tossing the pictures and all of that, but I just couldn't let you be satisfied with second best."

I hung my head and looked for a hole to crawl into. I thought of making a hasty exit, but instead I took two steps toward him and raised my arms. For a second I thought about hugging him, but I stopped myself and awkwardly placed both hands in my pockets. "Well, I've got to go home and have my dinner."

His reply surprised me. "I've got a pot of spaghetti cooking upstairs. I'm sure there's enough for two if you'd like to stay."

I wanted to say yes. "Spaghetti's my favorite food, but . . ."

"Okay, maybe some other time," said Mr. Roberts as he started to go upstairs to his apartment.

"I can call home and check anyway."

Mr. Roberts must have had ESP or something because when I joined him upstairs, a place had already been set for me. "Mom said okay."

The room was a combination den and eating area. There were two open doors on the wall to my left that led to a closet and a bathroom. On the far wall was a closed door I figured opened into a bedroom.

"This is pretty nice up here."

"Thanks," he replied as he scooped a big pile of spaghetti onto my plate. "It's just the right size for me. It gets a little crowded, though, when my son comes east to visit. Want some sauce?"

I nodded. A son. That was news to me. I mixed in the sauce and dug in. Everything tasted good. I wondered, What does Mr. Roberts's son look like? How old is he? Does he take pictures too? I twirled the next mouthful endlessly on the end of my fork.

"What are you thinking about?" asked Roberts.
"Huh?"

"I can smell the wood burning. What are you thinking about?"

"Nobody told me you had a son."

Mr. Roberts finished chewing before he answered. "I have a son who's seventeen. He lives with my ex-wife on the Coast."

"Is he in college?" The questions were forming quicker than I could ask them.

"No, a senior in high school. He had to repeat a year when he moved. He'll be going to college next year."

"How often do you get to see him?"

Mr. Roberts stared at the far wall, and his reply was low and difficult to hear. "Not enough. No, not enough at all. I'd like to see him more but . . . it just doesn't work out that way."

Spaghetti fell off my fork. I fought to catch it but it landed on the table.

"No it doesn't," I said. Then the fork slipped out of my hand and the end fell right into a pile of sauce on my plate. I wanted to cry suddenly, but I heard Mr. Roberts start to say something though I couldn't make out what it was.

"You know . . ." he said, finally loud enough for me to hear clearly, "it's hard when a family breaks up."

"I know," I replied softly, and then in a louder, almost irritated tone asked, "Did my mother tell you?" I twirled my fork faster. She had no right to do that but somehow I was glad she did.

Mr. Roberts poured some soda into my cup. "I've known about it since September."

"I don't think about it much."

Mr. Roberts flashed a disbelieving smile. "Tell me how you do that. It's been over seven years and I still think about it."

"It's much harder on my mom. She still looks for mail from him every day. He works long hours. I guess he doesn't have time to write. Sometimes I catch her sitting by the phone crying. I think she still misses him."

"Do you miss him?"

"Not really. Maybe a little. He was hardly ever at home even when he was at home. You don't miss what you never had." I glanced over Mr. Roberts's shoulder at the clock on the wall. "I've got to get home. It's late."

"You hardly ate."

I pushed my chair away from the table and stood up. "I had plenty. Thanks." Plenty, I thought, especially about that subject.

"I was going to put on a video of a great jungle movie. Can't you stay for that?"

"I have a lot of homework to do. Maybe some other time." Mr. Roberts walked me downstairs to my bike. Neither of us said a word.

I climbed on my bike and coasted down the driveway. Just before I got to the street, I stopped and looked back. I could see the occasional glow of Mr. Roberts's pipe in the darkness. "Thanks again!" I yelled, but I'm not sure he heard it. Then I headed home.

CHAPTER
SEVEN

December at Cinekyd started off with a special Friday night meeting. The podium microphone squealed as Mr. Roberts tapped the end with his finger. He waited until there was complete silence. "Those of you who are new probably wonder why I called this special meeting tonight." He took two Magic Markers from his pocket and wrote in big letters on an easel beside him EACH ONE in red and below it, in green, REACH ONE. Eugene and I looked at each other and shrugged. "As the end of each year approaches, a small tree appears at the back of the audion. At first it is bare, but as the season progresses the little tree begins to sprout ornaments—blue and red, silver and gold. Each of those ornaments stands for someone's love."

"Hey," whispered Eugene, "next time you go out with a girl give her one dozen Christmas tree ornaments to show her how much you love her."

"Why don't you make like a tree and leave," I replied.

"Every year," continued Mr. Roberts, "our local Children's Aid Society forwards us a list that represents the wishes of all the children under the society's care. We at Cinekyd fashion an annual event that tries to raise money to buy gifts for the less fortunate at holiday time."

Mr. Roberts paused to underline in black the slogan he had written on the easel. "Our campaign begins tonight. Ask your parents, grandparents, relatives, and friends for a donation. Five dollars buys a red ball; ten, a blue one; twenty, a silver one; and twenty-five or more gets a gold one. The more money we raise, the more children can benefit. Our campaign will run until December twenty-third. At that time we'll tally up all the money we've received and make the wishes of those disadvantaged children come true. Any questions?"

The idea of raising money to help other kids out really seemed like a neat idea. Maybe that was a way for a wimp to push his weight around. "Wouldn't it be great if we could raise a lot of money for this?" I whispered to Eugene. He nodded. "I mean a whole lot."

"I wouldn't mind selling cookies or hoagies or candy or cake or sundaes or breads or . . ."

"Selling or eating?" I asked. "If we did that, we'd have to donate you to the Children's Aid Society instead of the money. Maybe you'd be round enough to hang from the tree."

"Maybe we could rob the rich and give the money to the poor. Are you any good at archery?"

"Sure. Put an apple on your head and I'll show you how good I am. Seriously, we have to come up with something original. Something that has to do with families and with what we do here at Cinekyd. Something that— Hey, wait a minute. Let's meet here after this is over. I think I have a great idea." The idea was pure genius.

I waited until the audion was completely empty. "Christmastime is a family time, but sometimes because of distance or money or something, families can't be together. What if we went to people's houses with the portable video equipment and made a two-minute video of them, that they could send to their relatives. It would be like being there when they couldn't be there. We could call it a . . . a . . . video Christmas card. What do you think?"

"That's a great idea," said Big Eugene. "Count me in."

"Great, then we're off to Mr. Roberts's office so you can ask him if it's okay."

"Yep . . . Hey, wait! Why should I be the one to ask him? It's your idea."

"That's why I wanted *you* to ask him. Then it'll be both our ideas."

Eugene looked puzzled. "But I still don't know why I should be the one to do this."

I abruptly stopped and folded my hands. "If you're too chicken to do it, I'll do it myself."

"Okay," said Eugene as he paused to let me get in front of him. "I'll be right behind you if you forget anything."

It's not supposed to work this way. Usually when you call someone chicken, they agree to do it. "But—" I replied as he nudged me toward Roberts's office door.

"I'll jump in if you get stuck," said Eugene.

Eugene gave me the last bump that forced me into Mr. Roberts's office. There was no turning back. Mr. Roberts looked up from his writing and asked, "What's all the noise about? Can I help you guys with something?"

"Well," I said hesitantly, "We'd, ah, like, ah, to ah, make ah, . . . ah . . ."

"A video Christmas card," continued Eugene, "to raise money for the Children's Aid Society." Mr. Roberts looked puzzled. "You know, go into people's houses and videotape a Christmas message or greeting. Then they could send it to a friend or relative for Christmas."

"It would be just like, ah, being there when they couldn't be there," I added.

Mr. Roberts stood up from his desk and looked over at Eugene and then me. He shook his head and took a puff on his pipe that seemed to last forever. "A video Christmas card." I looked at Eugene out of the corner of my eye and then back at Roberts. It was impossible to tell what he was thinking. In another minute his serious expression dissolved into a smile. "You'll need one of the portable video recorders and the minicamera, two lights, a mike, a few clever ideas, and some videotape."

"You like the idea?" we said simultaneously.

The smile was bigger now. "Like it? Why, I think it's a great idea."

I was so happy, I grabbed Eugene by the arms and we both danced around in a circle and cheered. It probably looked pretty stupid, us jumping around and yelling like that, but we couldn't help ourselves.

Somewhat out of breath, I turned to Mr. Roberts and said, "I figure we could set up one video a night during the week, two on Friday and five on Saturday and Sunday. Whew, I still can't believe it. In ten days we could shoot about twenty-five. Do you really mean it?" He nodded his approval again. "You do. I can see you do. That would still give us a weekend to do the editing."

"And delivering," chimed in Eugene, "so that they could be sent out in plenty of time to arrive for Christmas."

Mr. Roberts shook both our hands. "Good luck."

Eugene and I slapped palms. We were in the video Christmas card business. Wait till Roberts saw how much money we raised. He was going to be very proud of me—I mean us.

CHAPTER
EIGHT

Eugene and I met the next day in the back of the audion. "I've been thinking about this project and we have a problem."

"We do?"

"We have someone who can work the lights, that's you, and we have someone who can hold the mike, that's me, but neither of us knows how to work the video camera or recorder."

"That's no problem," said Eugene. "We can ask one of the kids on the mobile video crew to help us."

"Who would you suggest asking?"

Eugene shrugged. "I don't know anybody on that crew."

"Neither do I, so we have a problem."

"Can't we just go up to the mobile video room and ask one of the kids if they want to help?"

"Great idea," I said. "It's your turn, though, to do the talking."

Big Eugene pointed to himself. "How did it get to be my turn. I did all the talking last time."

"That's true, but it was really supposed to be my turn so it's your turn this time."

"Oh, I get it," said Eugene. "It's my turn but you'll do all the talking!"

"Not really," I replied. "When it's my turn you do the talking but when it's your turn you do the talking too. See?"

"Ohhh. I get it. So it's my turn to talk this time." Eugene took two steps before it hit him. "Hey, wait! That means I talk either way."

"Okay, have it your way. When it's your turn you talk and when it's my turn you can talk too. Fair?" Eugene nodded. "Okay, let's go."

"Somehow that doesn't sound right," mumbled Eugene as he led the way reluctantly to the mobile video room. When he got to the door, he peeked inside and quickly took a step backward. "There's only a girl in there."

"So?" I replied, realizing that I wasn't much better in these situations.

"There's a tall girl with long red hair in there."

"So?"

"There's a tall girl with long red hair in there and she's . . . she's in there and . . . breathing and moving and . . . Listen, it's almost time for my dinner. Maybe we can ask somebody to help us the next time we're here."

Placing my hands on my hips, I said, "Are you going to do this to me again?"

"Me do this to you?" he snapped back. "You're the one that didn't want to talk last time."

I motioned to Eugene and he followed me to the end of

the hall. We had to have a serious wimp-to-wimp talk. "Do you still want to do this?"

Eugene chuckled. "Are you kidding? Of course I do."

"Then do it! If you get stuck, I'll jump in. Don't worry, I'm right behind you." It was then I had an amazing revelation. Whenever Big Eugene was supposed to do something, I was the one with the courage, and when it was my turn, he was the brave one. If we could only figure out a way to reverse things.

Cautiously, Eugene approached the door and we quietly tiptoed into the room. A girl was sitting at a table across the room, her back to us, working intently with an editing machine. Big Eugene cleared his throat loudly.

"Will you stop bothering me already," the girl snapped as she twirled herself around in the chair. "I told you that I— oh, sorry, I thought you were Roger." With that greeting I was mighty glad I wasn't Roger. "He's been in here four times already today asking me when I'd be . . . but you're not Roger, are you?"

Eugene took two steps backward and in the process managed to step on both of my feet. "You wouldn't want to help us, would you."

The girl looked first at Eugene and then at what she could see of me, behind him. "What don't you want me to do?"

"We need someone to work the video camera and recorder for us. You're not interested in doing it, are you."

The girl stood up and took a step toward Eugene as he continued his retreat. She was in the head-taller category that I was so used to.

I leaned a little more to the left so I wasn't so hidden. "What he means," I explained, "is that we need someone to work the video camera for us because, uh, we're doing a, ah, video Christmas card and, uh, we need, uh, someone to run the video camera for us for our video Christmas card. Understand?"

Eugene turned and faced me. "Don't you mean that we need someone to run the video camera for us when we do our video Christmas cards to raise money for the Children's Aid Society?" I nodded. "Then why didn't you just say that?"

I shook my head. "I did say that! You're the one that's got her all confused."

Eugene folded his arms. He was mad. "If you think you can ask her better than I, why didn't you do it in the first place?"

"It was your turn. Remember?"

The girl glanced at me, then back at Eugene, and without any warning got up grabbed a video camera off the shelf and walked out of the room. Bewildered, we stood there in silence until Eugene pounded his fist on the counter. "See what you did? Now she's never going to help us."

"What I did!" I replied, pounding my fist back in return. It's amazing how brave two wimps can be when they're yelling at each other. "You were the one that said she wouldn't want to help us and wasn't interested in helping us. Don't blame me."

"Yes, but you were the one that asked her if she would run the video camera for us for our video Christmas card."

We were eyeball to eyeball. "And what's wrong with that?"

"Outside of the fact that the sentence was long and re-petitive and convoluted and confusing and had seven mil-lion *uh*'s, it was fine," said Eugene.

"What's the difference now anyway? She's gone and

we've got no one to run the camera. . . . Shh. What's that?" It sounded like a machine running.

"What?" asked big Eugene.

"Shh, listen. Do you hear something?"

"Like a whirring sound?" asked Eugene.

"Like a motor running or—" Turning around together, we saw the red-headed girl just outside the doorway with a video camera in her hand taking pictures of us arguing. I covered my face with my hands and blurted out, "What are you doing with that camera? Are you crazy?" Eugene's body turned to stone and his mouth slowly dropped open, giving a clear shot of his tonsils.

Without a word of explanation, the girl put down the camera and took a tape out of a portable recorder that was hooked up to the camera. She walked across the room to two video decks sitting side by side on a worktable and placed the newly recorded tape in the deck on the right. At the flick of a switch two TV monitors in front of her came alive and Eugene and I watched an instant replay of ourselves fighting in stereo.

After watching it twice, the girl took another tape, placed it into the next deck, and began to transfer stuff from one to the other. After twenty minutes of this and adding music, she pointed to the second monitor. "Watch this, guys."

Following a symphonic introduction from the "1812 Overture" complete with cannons blasting in the background, the screen came alive with a picture of me pounding my fist on the table. "Would you," I said—now the tape cut to Eugene—"run the camera for us?" It was his turn now to pound the table followed by more cannons. The scene then cut back to me. "It would help us with"—and back to Eugene—"our video Christmas card."

"Were we being filmed the whole time we were here?"

Wendy nodded. "I had this camera on as an experiment." Eugene and I whistled and gave the girl a standing "O." She bowed. "Will you help?" we both asked.

"Tell me more about your project."

I opened my mouth to explain, but Eugene beat me to it. "I was trying to think of a way to raise a lot of money for Children's Aid this year and I . . ." Eugene paused and looked over at me. "I mean, we thought up this great idea for raising big bucks. We thought . . ."

As Eugene talked his eyes made their way down the redheaded girl's torso, pausing briefly to acknowledge her eyes doing the same to him but from the floor up. She was really cool. Too tall for me but just the right size for Eugene. I liked the way her shiny red hair hung down over her shoulders, almost reaching the belt of her jeans. Her eyes sparkled. I hoped she'd say yes.

"That's the whole story," concluded Eugene. His eyes were making a second trip. "If you don't want to help us . . ."

The girl smiled. "Of course I'll help you. By the way, my name's Wendy. What's yours?"

"I'm Eugene and that's Eugene. You can call me You and you can call him Gene."

"Wait a second. Don't anybody leave." In a minute I returned with three cans of Coke. "Here's," I said, raising my can high in the air, "to W E Squared Productions."

"W E Squared Productions?" they asked.

"Wendy Eugene squared, get it, two Eugenes?" Our cans clicked. The partnership had officially begun.

CHAPTER
NINE

The following Monday was the shooting of the first video and I wanted the whole world to know it. I planned to somehow carry two big lights, a microphone and cable bag, a video recorder, and a camera around school with me.

Mom peered over the morning paper. "Where in the world are you going with all that stuff?"

"We're shooting the first Christmas card video today after school." That was true. "We promised the people we'd be at their house no later than three-thirty." That was half true. Eugene had told them we'd be there between three-thirty and four. "If I have to come here to get the equipment, we'll be late." My plan was to take the equipment to school. This was my chance to become famous.

"Can't you call the people and see if you can push it back fifteen minutes?" She's always so logical.

"I didn't set this one up. Eugene did, so I have to take the stuff with me."

"Where are you going to put all that equipment?"

"In my locker."

"In your locker? It won't all fit in your locker."

"It'll fit it in and whatever doesn't I'll . . . I'll just carry it around."

My mother put her paper down on the table and shook her head. "Carry it around? Why, you'll look . . ." I think she was going to say ridiculous or stupid because she always says that, but she paused and instead finished with ". . . you'll maybe lose the stuff or break it."

This time I knew she was wrong. I pictured exactly how it would go. I'd be surrounded by a group of kids, possibly fifteen or twenty, and they'd be firing questions at me in rapid succession. . . . "Yes, the boy in the back with the ripped sweatshirt." "Eugene, what is that thing in the black case?" "Good question. Why, this is a digital high fidelity HQ recording deck." "Yes, the gorgeous girl in the back with the pretty smile." "What does the HQ stand for?" "Why the HQ stands for . . . ah . . . ah, high quintessence . . . it's a technical term that only means something to videographers. . . ."

"Mom, you just don't understand. I won't lose anything. Besides, it's probably safer if I keep my eyes on it the whole day anyway."

She shook her head and went back to reading the paper. "I may be a little late for dinner tonight because I don't know how long the video will take to shoot, this being the first time."

A hand appeared from behind the paper and waved. "I'll wait." Then the paper dropped and she gave me a warm smile. "Good luck."

I sort of ran all the way to the bus and hopped on. That's

when the real questions began. "What are you, some kind of secret agent with all that equipment?"

"Secret agent," said another kid from the back of the bus. "He's the mini-man with the Minicam!"

"You don't have to worry about people smiling when you take their pictures," chimed in another. "All they have to do is look at you!"

I sank down as low as I could in my seat and stared out the window. I had become an expert in pretending not to care. You have to sometimes, if you want to survive. The comments during the day were not much better.

After school I had a half hour to kill before Wendy's mom came, so I walked down to the wrestling room to say hello to Dan. If anyone would appreciate this stuff, it would be him. I opened the door to the room and poked my head in. The familiar Eau De Boys' Locker Room permeated my nostrils. I didn't see Dan at first, so I walked in and looked around. Scattered over the faded blue mats were boys of all shapes and sizes warming up. I stood off in the corner and pretended to take pictures.

"Hey, Shorty," yelled one of the guys from across the room, "what you got in that pocketbook?" As I looked up the words *Hey Todd do we have a match today?* flashed through my mind. The match had been a wrestling match. "Hey, Shorty," said Todd. "What do you have in that pocket-book?"

I could feel every muscle in my body tightening. "Are you talking to me?" I asked meekly.

Todd walked slowly toward me. "You're the only shorty with a pocketbook I can see here." A few guys stopped their warm-ups and started to laugh. "What you got in that pocketbook?"

"This," I replied, pointing to the video recorder, "is a video recorder. This is the camera that goes with it."

"Let me see the camera." I took a step backward but hit the wall. "Give it to me!"

"*No!*" The authority in my answer surprised me.

"You have thirty seconds to give it to me or I'm coming over to take it."

Reluctantly I handed it to him. "Be careful. It's fragile."

"It is?" he joked, pretending to drop it. All eyes were on us.

I wanted to punch him in the mouth. "Give me that back," I snapped.

Todd stood still and sneered. "If you want it, come and take it if you can." I lunged forward and tried to grab the strap, but he jerked it away. The room was filled with laughter. "What's the matter? Having problems?"

This time I swung at his face with my free hand. I wasn't even close, and to make matters worse the force of my blow spun me around and I dropped the other equipment I was carrying. My face felt hot and I yelled, "Come on, give it to me already, you jerk!" I was so angry, I almost burst out . . . crying. Somehow I held it in.

As I bent down to get the lights and microphone, Todd dangled the camera high above my head. "Anyone here think I should give this camera back?"

Everyone in unison yelled, "*No!*"

"Are you sure?"

"*Yes!*"

"Should I throw it out the window?"

"*Yes!*"

"Why don't you give him the camera back, Todd," said a stern voice from behind. Standing in the doorway was Dan. His face was bright red and the veins in his neck looked as if they were going to explode. Everyone froze and then scattered back to their mats to continue their warm-ups. Without saying anything else Dan marched across the room toward Todd.

Todd handed me the camera and started backing away across the mat. "It was only a joke, Coach. I wasn't going to do anything to him or the camera."

I cradled the equipment in my arms and ran out of the room. I didn't stop until I was safely in the parking lot. I was beginning to think I was a member of the humiliation-of-the-month club.

Out of breath and still somewhat terrified, I sat down on the curb to wait. My big day had become a big mess. One day, Todd whatever-your-name-is, I thought, one day . . . The picture was becoming much clearer. I would meet an Okinawan gardener and he would teach me— A beeping horn and Wendy hanging out the window of a red Chevrolet brought me back to earth.

She jumped out of the car and opened the back door for me. "Isn't all that equipment heavy to carry around?"

"Naw," I replied, thinking it wasn't the weight of the equipment that was the problem. "It doesn't weigh very much."

"Eugene, this is my mom." I looked up from arranging the equipment on the backseat and forced a smile.

"Excited about today?" asked Wendy's mom. I nodded. "So is Wendy. That's all she talks about now. It's video Christmas card this and Cinekyd that."

Wendy looked a little embarrassed. "Mom, I do not."

I was glad the two of them started jabbering back and forth, because I didn't feel much like talking to anybody. Maybe I would fix a flat tire for the world heavyweight wrestling champion and in repayment he would . . .

CHAPTER
TEN

Eugene was sitting on the grass next to his bike waiting for us as we pulled into the driveway. He ran over to the car and helped me carry the equipment up to the front door while Wendy arranged for her mom to pick us up later.

"Nervous?" asked Eugene.

"A little," I replied, still not able to get the wrestling-room scene completely out of my mind.

"These people are friends of your parents?" asked Wendy.

"I think they're friends of friends of friends of my parents, and are they loaded! Take a look at this house."

It appeared to be at least three stories high and there were too many windows to count. Big marble lions stood on either side of the doorway, and a solid gold plate in the middle of the door said *Ambrose.*

"I wonder if Steven Spielberg had a stomachache before

he shot his first film," asked Eugene as he pushed the bell. Loud melodic chimes, playing the first few bars of some classical piece twice, announced our presence. After a minute Eugene pushed the bell again, this time knocking on the door in rhythm to the chimes.

"Are you sure the people are expecting us today?" asked Wendy.

Eugene nodded and put his ear up to the door to listen. Suddenly he jumped back and pushed me to the front. "It's your turn to talk, remember?"

"It's my turn, but you're supposed to—"

"Not this time. You talk."

I could see there was no way out, so I moved to the front. If I can show a little courage each day, maybe I can dewimp myself. After what had just happened, now was a perfect time to start. Then I heard the barking and growling on the other side of the door. Maybe I'll start tomorrow, I thought. It's much better to start in the morning. I took a step backward just as the door opened.

"Can I help you?" asked a skinny gray-haired man. Behind him were two black growling Dobermans.

In my highest, squeakiest voice I replied, "I think we're in the wrong place."

The skinny man looked down at the video camera and motioned for us to come in. "You must be the kids from that video place."

"Cin-n-n-nekyd?" I stuttered.

"That's it, Cinekyd. I'm Mr. Ambrose. The rest of my family is waiting for you in the den."

I smiled nervously at both dogs, who were still growling, and pointed to Eugene. "The fat guy behind me is a lot tastier. May I suggest the rump cut?"

Mr. Ambrose chuckled. "Come on in. They won't hurt

you." They may eat you, I thought, but after the first few bites it doesn't hurt at all. I cautiously took a step inside. "Follow me. The den's just down the hall and to the right."

With widened eyes and dripping fangs my snarling escorts matched me step for step into the den. This is the end to a perfect day, I thought. First I'm humiliated in school, then I'm nearly beaten up in the wrestling room, and now the odds are eight to five that I'll be the gourmet main course for these two dogs.

A pretty gray-haired woman and twins were sitting in front of a fireplace at the far end of the room. "The kids from the video place are here," said Mr. Ambrose.

"It'll take us about fifteen minutes to set up," replied Eugene bravely from the back.

"Grrrr." The three of us stood frozen, clutching our equipment, in the center of the room. "Grrrrrrr."

"Tiny and Walter, cut that out!" snapped Mr. Ambrose. "Get over here now." The growling stopped as the dogs' tails dropped between their legs and they lay down by the fireplace.

When we finished setting up, I said with some authority, "Okay, how about if everybody moves in a little closer together?"

"Okay, how about if everybody moves in a little closer together?" repeated a high-pitched nasal voice from behind.

I gave Eugene a dirty look. Didn't he know this was not the time to play games? "Here's what I want you to do now," I said, turning my attention back to the family.

"Here's what I want you to do now."

"Cut it out already, Eugene!" I mouthed silently. "Don't joke around."

Big Eugene looked puzzled as he exclaimed, "Cut out what?"

"Cut out what?" the voice echoed.

Wendy pointed to the opposite corner of the room. There, perched on the back of a chair, was one of the largest multicolored parrots I had ever seen. I put my finger up to my lips. "Shh." The parrot cocked its head to the side and from where I was, it looked like it shook its head no and smiled.

Turning back to the family, I said, "When I drop my hand you . . ."

"When I drop my hand you . . ."

". . . look at me, not at the camera."

". . . look at me, not at the camera."

"Will you shut up already," I said in disgust.

"Will you shut up already," the parrot repeated with a twinkle in its eyes.

"There's nothing we can do about Gabby," said Mr. Ambrose. "He repeats everything anyone but us says and he's impossible to catch. After you finish your instructions everything will be fine."

"Okay," I said quickly and in a mumble. "Startgiving-yourmessageaChristmasgreetinganythingyoumightwantto-saytoyourrelatives. WhenIdropmyhandsstarttalking."

"Okay," the parrot repeated slowly, with perfect enunciation, "start giving your message, a Christmas greeting, anything you might want to say to your relatives. When I drop my hand start talking. *Brawk! Brawk!*"

I motioned for Eugene to turn on the light and for Wendy to start the camera. "Ambrose video, take one," but instead of dropping my hand I waited for Gabby to talk. Instead there was silence. Half an hour later we had enough footage to make a terrific two-minute video.

"When will the video be ready?" asked Mr. Ambrose.

"We'll deliver the finished product to you in about ten days," replied Big Eugene as we started to pack up our stuff.

"We'll deliver the finished product to you in about ten days," repeated Gabby, who was now flying furiously around the room above us.

On our way out Tiny and Walter followed us to the entrance of the foyer and stopped. Gabby, on the other hand, followed us all the way, settling down to rest on a plant that hung by the door.

As Wendy opened the door I stopped and eyeballed the parrot. "You know something, Gabby? You were a real pain in the butt today. Is that all you can do? Just repeat what other people say? Huh?" Wendy and Eugene looked at me like I was crazy. I tipped an imaginary hat to Gabby and sneered. "Guess I told you, all right?"

Gabby sat there in silence. His smile was gone. I had won. At least my day was going to end in a victory. Suddenly, Gabby began to flap his wings furiously and flew straight up to the ceiling, where he began circling the room. When he got to the spot where Walter and Tiny were resting, he dived down, landing on the floor beside them. He looked over at the three of us and then, in his loudest, clearest voice, yelled, "Sic 'em! Sic 'em!"

Walter and Tiny jumped up and, fangs showing, charged over in our direction. The three of us flew out the door, slamming it behind us with a crash. We hid in the bushes at the end of the drive until Wendy's mom came to get us.

"Well, how did your first video go?" she asked.

"Not bad," said Wendy.

"Not bad," I repeated.

"Not bad," parroted Eugene. And we all broke up laughing.

CHAPTER
ELEVEN

In all, W E Squared Productions made twenty-six videos. I secretly made one for myself. We planned to celebrate our success on Saturday at the Cinekyd Christmas party.

The audion was half filled when I arrived that night. I saw Andi, but I stood off to the side to wait for Eugene and Wendy. There was no way I could ever face her again. Besides, I thought, she's jabbering away over there with Dan . . . I think she just spotted me . . . she didn't . . . I'm safe . . . or did she? You think you see me over here but it's not me.

"Hi. Haven't seen you around school lately. Where've you been hiding?"

"I . . . Well, you see . . . The other day, I mean for the past month . . . It's like this . . . understand?"

Andi shook her head. "That certainly clears up everything. Did you ever consider running for political office?"

"What I really wanted to say was, I've been very busy with my schoolwork . . . not really that busy, but busy enough to not be able to . . . but that's not every day. On certain days, mostly Tuesday and Thursday, no Monday and Wednesday, but not every week . . . Okay?" I scanned the room for Eugene and Wendy.

Andi was trying not to smile. "That's what I thought. Is this your first Christmas party here at Cinekyd?" I nodded as I continued to look. "Who are you looking for?"

"Eugene and Wendy. They're supposed to be here already." I shifted my weight from my left foot to my right and back, thankful that I didn't get motion sickness. "So, this is my first Christmas party here at Cinekyd."

Andi started to laugh. "I know."

"You do?" I replied. "How did you know?"

"You just told me."

"I did?" Now I started to laugh just as someone tapped me on the shoulder.

"What's up?" It was Eugene.

"Hey, I was looking all over for you. Did you just get here?"

"Yep. Have you seen Wendy yet?"

"Not yet. Oh, by the way, Eugene, this is . . . Ah . . . this is . . ." The first name with the *i* on the end had disappeared again. "Eugene this is . . ." and with my head down I mumbled "memyem" praying that Eugene would say "What?" and the girl would fill in her name. Instead, Eugene and girl stared at each other in silence. Please, I prayed, say your name.

"Nice to meet you, Memyem," said Eugene, extending his hand. "I've seen you behind the cameras Wednesday nights. I didn't know your name was Memyem."

"Andi," replied the girl nonchalantly.

"Andi Memyem. Do you have an older brother?" Andi shook her head no. I turned away so Eugene couldn't see me beginning to laugh. It was good to have the spotlight away from me. "I think there was a boy with that last name on my little League Team a couple years ago."

"Hi, Andi, Hi, Eugenes," said Wendy, who seemed to appear from nowhere. "What's so funny?"

"Nothing," I replied. The lights were beginning to dim. "You got here just in time. I think Mr. Roberts is ready to start. Let's sit down over there."

A gold spotlight followed Mr. Roberts and fifteen Cinekyd staff members carrying plastic bags filled to the brim with toys up to the front of the audion and onto the stage. The edges of Mr. Roberts's smile met in the back of his head. Puffing out his chest, he began, "This year has been the most successful fund-raising drive in the history of Cinekyd. Just look at the bags and bags of toys we" he said, pointing to the people standing behind him, "were able to buy for the needy children in our community. Everyone worked very hard for this project and I thank you all for this. I'd also like to give a special thanks to three of our members who raised six hundred seventy-five dollars with their video Christmas card. Lets give a rousing hand of applause to the two Eugenes, and Wendy."

Everyone stood up and clapped. Mr. Roberts came off the podium and shook each of our hands. When he got to me, he squeezed my hand extra hard and gave me a pat on the back. I felt like jumping up and down and yelling, *"All right!"* Not just because we raised $675 and helped all those kids, but because Mr. Roberts thought we did a good job. *All right!* I yelled inside silently. *All right!* It felt good being appreciated.

70

My mother was up in bed reading when I got home. "How was the party?" she asked.

I sat down on the edge of the bed. "It was great. We raised more money this year than ever before and W E Squared Productions raised the most of any single group."

"That's quite an accomplishment. Now aren't you glad I made you go there the first day?" My mother smiled and returned to reading her book, not really expecting me to answer.

"Mom, can I ask you a question?" I had struggled with this moment for days.

She rested her book on her lap again. "Sure. What is it?"

"Do you know where Dad is now?"

My mother shut her book and sat up. Her head hung down and there were tears in her eyes. I was not surprised by her reaction. "I haven't heard from him for over six months, but I'll give the last address I have. Are you going to write to him?"

"Sort of. I wanted to send him something. Can you give it to me now?"

I thought she might ask me a few more questions, but instead she just said, "It's in the top drawer in the desk in the kitchen."

"Do you think he'll write back?" I didn't know if I wanted her to answer truthfully or not. I could tell she didn't know how to answer either.

"I think he'll probably answer you," she finally said.

I gave her a hug and went downstairs to the den, where I put on the TV. I searched for a tape I had hidden in the cabinet a few days before, and when I found it, I put it in the video recorder.

At first there were just black-and-white flickers with static, but this faded into a picture of the outside of my house. I narrated in the background. "Hi, Dad, It's me. Thought it was a good idea to bring you up-to-date about what's happening in my life. This is the outside of our new house. It's not as big as our old one, but it's okay." The scene then switched to my room. "This is my room. I thought about cleaning it up, but then you wouldn't believe it was my room. In case you're wondering, I'm taking these pictures with a video camera. Mom got me hooked up at this place called Cinekyd and there is this great guy, Mr. Roberts, that runs it. I'm learning how to take photographs and shoot videos and maybe when you come to visit I'll take you over to see the place." The camera swung around and focused on my pillow. Then I appeared. "I don't know if I'm in focus or not. I hope I am. How do I look?" I stood up on the bed. "Say taller, please!" Then I flopped down. There was a brief pause and I remembered having a difficult time thinking of things to say. "Dad, I wish you were home for the holidays, but since you can't be I guess this is the second best thing." Then I waved. "Happy holiday. Please write or call soon. . . . Mom and I miss you a lot." The black-and-white lines and static appeared again.

I rewound the tape and wrapped it in a double layer of brown paper. After addressing the package and putting on lots of postage, I put it outside in the mailbox and went to sleep. When I got up the next day, the package was gone.

CHAPTER
TWELVE

I waited a couple weeks before I started checking the mailbox. Nothing came. He didn't call. I continued this ritual every day during January. I gave up my vigil the night of the second special meeting at Cinekyd.

As usual I sat down next to Eugene and Wendy. I joked. I smiled. I laughed louder than usual. I was doing just what Mr. Roberts wanted me to do. Acting.

I leaned over to Tommy, who was sitting in the row in front of me, and asked, "Is this about the summer movie?"

"That's my guess," he replied.

"You know the boss pretty well. What do you think the movie's going to be?"

Tommy smiled, as if he had some inside information. "Look, I don't know anything for sure, but last year we did a western and the year before that we did a space adventure. So my guess for this year is a horror movie."

Big Eugene jumped up with excitement. "A horror movie would be great. Can you just see me as Count Dracula?" With that he put his arm in front of his face and in his best Transylvanian accent bellowed, "I want to suck youze blood. What do you think? Were you scared to death?"

"You sounded like a vampire from Philadelphia," said Andi, who had just sat down next to me.

"If someone had snuck into my room," said Wendy, "and said that to me, I probably would have died . . . died laughing. I do think you show promise on the stage, though."

Eugene beamed. "You do?"

"There's one leaving in five minutes."

"Very funny," he replied. "Seriously, anyone here going to try out for a part?"

"I am," said Wendy. "I had a small part in last year's film. Maybe I can get a bigger part this year. What about you?" she asked, turning to me. "Are you trying out?"

"No. I can't act. I'll stick to taking the photos of the production."

"Everybody can act a little," chimed in Tommy. "You should try it sometime before the summer. You might surprise yourself."

"No way. You guys can stay in front of the camera. I'm just as happy to stay behind."

"That's the place for me too," said Andi.

"Hello! Hello!" Mr. Roberts tapped on the mike with his fingers. "Is this on? Can you hear me?" he asked.

"Yes!"

"Tonight," he continued, "I'd like to show you an old black-and-white 1930s feature film entitled *Tarzan Finds a Son*. Why, you may ask, is he showing us this and what does this have to do with the summer movie project? That, my friends, is what you have to figure out. Lights! Roll 'em."

I tapped Tommy on the shoulder. "A jungle horror movie?"

"Beats me," he replied.

The lights dimmed and the projector whirred behind me. I had seen Tarzan movies before on TV, but this one was a little different. Tarzan's son, Boy, seemed to be in more action scenes than Tarzan. In one scene he fought a lion with his bare hands and won. In another scene he stood in the path of a herd of wildly charging elephants and stopped them by beating his chest and making jungle sounds with his mouth.

The end of the movie had the best scene of all. Boy was walking through the jungle when an evil native chieftain jumped out of the bushes. Raising his spear, he bellowed, "Prepare to die." Boy tensed his muscles as he eyed the chieftain. Without any warning he yelled, "Ahahahahahahahahah!" and flattened the native with one punch. All right, Boy!

When the movie was over, Mr. Roberts asked, "Well? How'd you like it?" Everyone applauded. "Who knows why I showed this movie tonight? Wendy?"

"Because the movie this summer is going to be a jungle movie."

"Right," said Mr. Roberts. "The name of our movie will be *Simba the Wildling.*"

Big Eugene pounded his chest. "Do you think I look like a jungle boy?"

"A gorilla maybe," I replied. "But no jungle boy."

"The staff is going to pass out brochures," continued Mr. Roberts, "which have all the information you need to know about the summer program here at Cinekyd. Look them over now, and if anyone has any questions I'll try to answer them."

The brochure was bright yellow, and in bold black letters on the front it said:

SUMMER CINEKYD & SIMBA

Inside across from the workshop schedules was the following:

Bart Adams joins Professor JoAnne Hobson in their search for Simba the lost wildboy of the jungle. But sinister forces and jungle dangers await them as they travel through deepest darkest Africa.

When you join Cinekyd's summer video shops, you become part of an award-winning production team on the set of an exciting new television feature. You'll have a chance to act, to use professional video equipment, to create special effects, and to help make *Simba the Wildling.* When it's all over, hundreds of viewers will see your work at the Hollywood-style premiere. And thousands more will watch it on Cinekyd's cable TV network.

It sounded too good to be true. I could chronicle the production from beginning to end with photographs or design a program for opening night or both.

Or maybe I would try out for a small part. In my mind I saw myself as Simba . . . a little taller and with muscles of iron. . . . I'm walking along in the jungle with my monkey friend when all of a sudden a native, spear in hand, surprises me from the bushes. He looks an awful lot like Todd. "Moogamba wimp! Meeboo Shorty! Meeboo Shorty!"

"Who you sayin' Meeboo Shorty to, huh?" I yell.

"You!" replies the native. "What are you going to do about it?"

"This!" I reply as I grab the spear from his hand and break it in half. "And this! Ahahahahahahaha" I yell at the top of my lungs as I give him an airplane spin, a backbreaker, an African ear-crusher, and the Chinese pretzel twist. "If you ever call me Shorty again, I'll be forced to use the Manchurian flying dorsal body annihilator." From the ground Todd looks up at me with terror in his eyes. In a flash I climb up the nearest tree to look for a vine home—

"Hi, Gene." I looked up from the brochure. It was Mr. Roberts.

"Huh? Oh, I'm doing great." I emphasized the *great.*

"What do you think of the idea for the movie?" he asked.

"I can't wait for the summer to get here now. I already have ideas for pictures."

"Trying out for a part in the movie?" Mr. Roberts asked.

"Me? I can't act. I'll just stick to still photography."

"Think about it. Maybe you'll change your mind."

"Not me. This summer you'll find me behind the lens not in front of it." It's funny, though. Inside I was thinking something completely opposite. Maybe I'd try out for a small part. Hmm. I could be in a wild gorilla costume and no one would know it was me. Or I could be a native or someone on the street or a jungle boy swinging from tree to tree. I'd wave to the Boss with my left hand while I caught the vine with my right. He'd stand behind one of the cameras, chest all puffed out, a smile on his face, and would wave back. "See how easy it was!" he'd yell. Maybe I would try out for a part. . . .

CHAPTER
THIRTEEN

I thought a lot about Mr. Roberts's personal invitation to try out for a part in the movie. In fact, I found myself thinking less and less about my father and more about him. He made me feel good. He seemed to understand me. We were almost a team.

One Wednesday evening in late February I decided to take pictures while they shot *Dusty's Clubhouse,* a weekly comedy segment on Cinekyd Cable Theater.

I walked in just as Eric, one of the directors, hung up the phone. "He's sick all right. What are we going to do now?"

"Let's shoot everything but his part and splice it in later," suggested Tommy.

"That would be okay if we didn't have to have it ready for airtime tomorrow night," said Eric.

"If only we had someone to take David's place," said Andi.

"Who could we possibly get at such a late date?" asked Lee.

"Let's get started anyway," said Eric as he put his headset on. "Camera's ready? Decks ready? Actors ready? Five, four, three, two . . ."

I was just about to shoot a picture when someone tapped me on the shoulder. It was Mr. Roberts. "Have you ever seen an episode of *Dusty's Clubhouse* before?" he whispered.

I nodded. "I saw them practicing this episode last week. It's a riot." I raised my camera and started to take a few pictures.

"Where's David?" whispered Mr. Roberts.

"He sick," I replied.

"Who are they getting for his part?"

"They couldn't find anybody."

"I know someone who might be good," said Mr. Roberts.

I mouthed *Who?* and Mr. Roberts pointed to me.

I pointed to myself and shook my head no. Mr. Roberts shook his head vehemently yes. It was then that he motioned for me to follow him out of the studio. "Come on. Why don't you try it?" I continued to shake my head no.

"Give me one good reason why not," he persisted.

"Because I . . . I'm not a very good actor."

"How do you know?"

"I just know."

"Have you ever tried to act?"

"Not really."

Mr. Roberts smacked his pipe on the palm of his hand and let the ashes fall to the floor. "You know what your problem is, Eugene?"

I smiled nervously. "No."

"You're afraid to take a risk."

Why should I do something that might end up embarrassing me? Surely he could understand that. *I am not.*

"Then try it," he persisted.

"I don't want to." It felt like a tug of war.

"See what I mean? You are afraid."

I threw my hands up in surrender. "Okay, so I'm afraid."

But Roberts didn't quit. "What's the worst thing that could happen?"

What a dumb question. "I could mess up my lines."

"That's the beauty of video. If you mess up your lines, we'll shoot it over."

"The kids might laugh at me," I said.

"The kids might laugh with you."

"I might make a fool of myself."

"You might be a star. Can't you see the point? Every situation has at least two sides to it. If you never take a chance, you never give yourself an opportunity to see the other side, the good side."

He had a point there. "Even if I say yes, how could I learn all the lines?"

"If I make that easy for you," said Mr. Roberts, "will you do it?" I took a deep breath and slowly nodded yes. "Good, because there's no script."

I put both hands on my head. "No script?" This isn't risky, it's crazy!

"Don't get so excited," said Mr. Roberts. "First I'll tell you all about the character. Then I'll go over the lines with you. You don't have to learn them word for word. Just get the general idea. After a little practice you'll be set to go on." I took a long, slow, deep breath. What had I gotten myself into? "You're going to play a mad scientist, Professor Doctor Professor. Peggy will help you with your costume. Your cue to come on is just after Tommy says, 'I

know who that is.' Can you do a German accent?" I nodded. "Now here's *vat* you do . . ."

Twenty minutes later the cameras were rolling.

knock knock

"I know who that is."

The door to the clubhouse opened and there, dressed in a
white coat worn backward, a gray wig that didn't fit, and
oversize black glasses, was Professor Doctor Professor.
What a weird way to break into acting.

"Hello, Professor Doctor Professor."

"Vhy, hello, Duzty. Do you vant to help me in zis zien-
tific experiment?"

"Sure, Professor."

"Goot. Get a peeze of paper and a penzil and write down
exactly vat I tell you." Tommy got a piece of paper and
waited for me to continue. I opened my hands. "Zee dis?"
Tommy looked in. "Zis is zee grazzhopper. Now, pay attention." I pretended to put a grasshopper on the table.
"Zump!" I moved my head back and then quickly forward
to indicate it had jumped. "Okay, Duzty. Write 'Ven ve zay
zump, ze grazzhopper zumps.' Now, Duzty, I'm pulling ze
front legzs off like zis," and I pretended to pull off the front
legs and put the grasshopper back on the table. "Zump!"
Again I showed movement with my head. "Okay, Duzty.
Write 'Ven ve pull ze front legzs from ze grazzhopper and
zay zump, ze grazzhopper zumps!' Now Duzty, for the
cruzial part of ze experiment. Vatch az I pull ze back legz
off."

As I pretended to pull off the back legs, I looked in the
direction of Mr. Roberts for some indication of how I was
doing. Unfortunately, the lights were so bright, all I could
see was the periodic glowing of his pipe when he took a
puff. "Zump!" This time my head didn't move. "Zump!"

Again no sign of jumping. *"Zump! Zump!"* Waving my hands in wild excitement, I turned to Tommy. "Juzd zas zi zought. Duzty, write 'Ven you pull ze bak legz off ze grazzhopper, he becomez deaf." I waited for my critical review.

Initially there was complete silence. Then I heard a few scattered *oh, no*'s mixed with snickering and then . . . outright laughing. Eugene was the first to pat me on the back. Wendy and Andi followed with hugs. After that I couldn't tell where the congratulations were coming from. What a great feeling!

When the commotion was over, I looked around for Mr. Roberts. He was nowhere to be found. I went up stairs to tell him I was definitely trying out for the summer movie. As I approached his office it was unusually quiet. I knocked on the half-open door, and as it swung open I saw that he was not there either.

Piled in front of his desk was a large brown suitcase and draped over it was a matching wardrobe bag. I looked down the hall, and when I was sure no one was coming I walked over to the luggage. As I ran my hand slowly over the wardrobe bag to see if it was filled with clothes, a small white folder with red lettering that must have been under it fell to the floor. I picked it up and read the outside. WESTCOAST AIRWAYS. Inside was a ticket for a flight to San Francisco leaving at ten-thirty that evening and returning early Monday morning.

I smiled. I wondered if the visit was a surprise. Most likely it'd been planned for weeks and his son would meet him at the airport. I slipped the ticket back into the folder, and tucked it under the wardrobe bag where it had been before. What a lucky guy his son was.

Then I thought about the tape I had sent my dad. Why hadn't I gotten a letter? Why hadn't I gotten a phone call? I gritted my teeth and stomped around the room. "It's not fair! It's just not fair!"

When I got to Mr. Robert's suitcase, I gave it a karate kick. The suitcase landed on its side with a thump and the wardrobe went crashing into the desk. I stood completely still, surveying the mess, before I righted the suitcase. "I'm really not mad at you," I said as I held the wardrobe up in front of me. "You should visit your son, but my father should visit me too. It's just not fair." I rearranged the case so no one could tell anything had happened. "You'd visit me if you were my father," I mumbled to myself as I backed out of the room and right into Mr. Roberts.

Had he heard? "I was looking for you." I didn't think he had.

"I was getting something in the basement. What did you want?"

"I think I'm going to try out for a part in the summer movie."

"That's great. Listen, I'm a little rushed tonight. We can talk about it more next week."

"Have a . . ." I almost slipped and said *safe trip*, but I caught myself and said, "Good night." And then I disappeared downstairs.

CHAPTER
FOURTEEN

I'll bet he helped me with that part in *Dusty's Clubhouse* because he wants me to be Simba in the summer movie. I can understand why. Simba and I have a lot in common. We're both small and both have . . . well, we both can . . . I took off my shirt and flexed my muscles in front of my mirror. I was perfect for Simba the Weakling. The story would be about a family that purposely lost their kid in the jungle and nobody wanted to find him. If I was going to have a chance to be Simba the Wildling, I needed a way to build myself up.

That night I asked Mom to cook spaghetti, my favorite food. I always imagined that it made my muscles get bigger. Power food.

The next day after school I went down to the wrestling room to ask Dan for some kind of a workout program. Don't worry, I kept repeating to myself, Dan won't let anything happen to you. If you want to get anyplace in life, you have to take risks. There are always two sides to everything. You'll either get a workout program from Dan or a workout from Todd.

Nervously I opened the door a crack and scanned the room. Most of the wrestlers were warming up in a circle around the outside of the mats. A few scrimmaged in the center. Where was Dan? I gazed around the room one more time. Was Dan late again? I was just about to leave when an ice-cold hand clamped itself around my neck and straightened me up. My outstretched hands pushed open the gym doors as I was coaxed rudely forward. "Hey, Todd! Look who came to visit us!" yelled one of the wrestlers as he pushed me toward the center of the mat.

Todd, who was on his back doing sit-ups, looked up at me with a satisfied smile. "Come to learn some wrestling?" he asked with a chuckle. As he slowly stood up I realized he wasn't as tall as I originally thought he was.

"Not really," I timidly said as I started to back away. "I came to ask Dan something but I can come back another time."

"Not so fast!" he barked. If I could have run away as fast as my heart was beating, I would have been safe. Instead I froze. "Wanna learn how to wrestle?"

I smiled nervously. "Thanks anyway. Maybe some other time."

"Prepare to defend yourself." Todd crouched over like a gorilla and began waving his arms wildly from side to side. Still upright, I tried to protect myself by slapping his hands away when they came near. Todd began by slapping my sides and my legs. "You'd better crouch down like me or you'll be a dead duck." I bent my body over at the waist and held my arms out in front of me. The wrestlers who lined the mat began to roar with laughter.

Suddenly, Todd threw both his arms up into the air. Like a dope I watched them instead of Todd, and when I did he fell to his knees and slapped me on my left ankle with his right hand. "If we were really wrestling, you'd be flat on your face eating mat."

The laughter seemed to get louder. Todd got up from his crouch and started to circle me again. I began to feel dizzy as I spun around to keep track of him. I was close to throwing up.

"Dan's coming!" yelled one of the guys who had been watching the hall from the door. Everyone scattered to continue their warm-ups.

"Gene," asked a surprised Dan as he entered the gym and saw me still crouched over, trying to catch my breath all alone in the middle of the mat. "What are you doing here?"

I looked over first at Todd's face and then at his semiclenched fist. "I . . . came here . . . to ask you if . . ." I thought I heard someone behind me snickering. "Listen, ah, you're busy . . . so how about if I ask you about it . . . next week at . . ." and in a whisper I said, "Cinekyd."

"I'm so late already, a few minutes more won't make a difference. What can I do for you?"

"I wanted to ask you if—if— actually this is not for me, it's for Eugene." What would everybody think if they knew it was really for me? "Yeah, it's for Eugene." Repeating the sentence gave me time to collect my thoughts. "He wanted to be on some exercise program . . . you know, to lose some weight and build himself up. So he asked me, to ask you, if . . . you could write down a program for him to follow. You know, some exercises, some . . . whatever." The giggling continued.

Dan thought for a second. "How about if I give it to him myself when I see him next Wednesday? Is that okay?"

I was going to say, "That'll be fine," and back out of the room, when I realized that Dan would give Eugene an exercise program and he wouldn't know what it was all about. "You see, I, I mean he, wanted to get things started as soon as he could because . . . because he wants to get into the best shape possible before the summer." Then I threw in something that I knew Dan couldn't resist. "I think it has to do with some part he wants in the Simba movie."

"I don't really have time to do that justice now but . . ." Dan walked over to the large khaki duffel bag sitting in the corner of the room and began to rummage through it.

As I stood there all alone in the center of the wrestling gym, snickering to the left of me and snickering to the right, I realized why Eugene had lied to me. Wasn't I guilty of the same thing right now? I could no more tell Dan that the exercise program was for me than Eugene could have told me he was at Cinekyd for the first time. We were both afraid that if we told the truth, the other person might laugh at us. Sometimes you have to lie to protect yourself.

"You're in luck," said Dan. Smiling, he handed me two mimeographed sheets of paper. "Tell Eugene to follow the instructions exactly as they are on here. If he has any questions, he can ask me at Cinekyd."

I was so anxious to see what it said, I took the paper without even saying thanks and started to read it.

TRAINING SCHEDULE J.V. WRESTLING TEAM

Week 1   EXERCISES
             A. 20 push-ups (2 sets)

B. 40 sit-ups (3 sets)
C. 10 pull-ups
D. 100 toe raises

Weight Training (100 lbs. weight set)

"A hundred-pound-weight set?" I blurted out. "Where am I . . . I mean where is he . . . going to get a hundred-pound-weight set?"

"There's one in the basement at Cinekyd," yelled Dan as he motioned for the J.V. team to join him at the blackboard. "We used it for props in a movie we did a few years ago."

"All right!" I replied, jumping up into the air. And it was only then that I realized I was still standing in the middle of the mat. "Hey, Dan, I better be going. Thanks a lot. This is exactly what I . . . Eugene wanted. Thanks a lot." I bolted out of the wrestling room and didn't stop running until I was halfway home. Now to convince Eugene. You know the problem with you, Eugene. You're afraid to take risks.

CHAPTER
FIFTEEN

I was reading a fitness magazine outside the darkroom while I waited for some prints to dry when I heard Eugene tromping down the hall.

"Unbelievable. Absolutely unbelievable," I said in a loud, clear voice.

"What are you reading?" he asked.

I lowered the magazine so I could see him. "It's an article on physical fitness." I buried my face again. "It's nothing special."

"So what's doing?"

"That's amazing. I can't believe it. That can't be true."

Eugene stood directly in front of me and peered over the top of the magazine. "What's amazing? What can't you believe? What can't be true?"

I folded up the magazine and tossed it onto the table. "That article is so weird, I don't even want to waste your time with it."

"Okay," said Eugene. "So what's doing?"

I got up and opened the magazine one more time and pretended to read something. "No one in their right mind would believe that."

"What?" pleaded Eugene.

"This," I replied, pointing to the article.

"What?"

"This is what!"

Eugene waved his hands "This is what? What is this?"

"This dumb magazine article. Let me ask you a question. Do I look fit to you?"

"You're a little skinny but you look fit to me."

"That's what I thought, but this article is a physical fitness test and according to it not only am I unfit but I'm close to dead."

"Let me see the article."

Now I was in a little bit of a jam because there was no fitness article in this magazine. "You don't want to waste your time."

"Yes, I do!"

"No, you don't," I insisted. "Besides, it's nothing to see. It's a test you take to see how fit you are."

"Then give me the test."

"It's dumb and a waste of time."

"Who are you to tell me how I can spend my time!" Eugene's ears were bright red. "If I want to waste my time taking this test, then you can't stop me."

"Okay, but I warned you." I breathed a sigh of relief. I had Eugene right where I wanted him now. "Question one. How many sit-ups can you do?"

"I can do twenty," he replied without hesitation.

"Do it."

"What's the matter? Don't you believe me?"

"Sure I believe you. Do it."

Eugene lay down on the floor and began. "One, two, three . . ." Large beads of sweat rolled down his face and he puffed like an old horse with a lung condition. ". . . fifteen, six—" And he collapsed in a heap.

"Hmm. Sixteen. Okay. Can you touch the floor with your palms?"

"Easy!"

"Do it!"

Eugene bent over. His palms zoomed past his waist, slowed a little at his knees, and came to a screeching halt at his ankles. "Ennnnnnnnnnhhh." The veins on his neck bulged. "Ennnnnnnnnnnnhh." He was purple from the neck up. "Ennnnnnnhh." His palms didn't budge.

"I think you better stop before you blow a gasket. The answer to question two is no. Next. Can you jump rope for three minutes?"

"No."

"Can you do fifteen push-ups?"

"No."

"Lift eighty percent of your weight?"

"Are you kidding?"

"Can you run six hundred yards in two minutes?"

"No way."

"That's part one. Part two is just questions. Do you eat desserts more than twice a week?"

Eugene pointed to his stomach.

"I guess that's a yes. Do you ever snack?"

Eugene pointed again.

"Do you eat junk food?"

This time he smiled and shook his head no.

"Do you eat brussels sprouts, kale, Swiss chard, or fiddleheads?"

"No! No! No! and *No!"*

"Okay, let me tally up your score. Hmm. Carry the four. AAhhhh. Add the three. Ooooooowwwwww. According to this . . ."

"Yes? Well. How did I do?"

"You should check into a nursing home."

"Seriously. How'd I do?"

"It says here 'Trade in your body.' You're in as bad a shape as I am, but . . ." I paused for effect. "There is something we can do."

"What?"

"Forget it, you probably wouldn't want to do it."

"Do what?"

"It."

"What is it?"

"This!" And I pulled Dan's workout sheet out of my pocket.

Eugene studied it for a few minutes. "Can you keep a secret?"

"Sure," I replied.

"You have to promise never to tell anyone about this ever." Eugene looked more serious than I had seen him before. "Promise?"

"Promise," I replied, wondering what all this was leading up to.

"And you can't laugh at this either, understand?"

I think my impatience was beginning to show in the tone of my voice. "Have I ever laughed at anything you told me?"

"No," he whispered softly, pausing again to gather his courage. "You know, I always wanted to lift weights and work out with the guys, but I never did it."

"You did?"

"Weight lifting and working out was for the cool guys, the in-guys. I've always been an outie. Even from the day I was born." Eugene lifted up the front of his shirt and pointed to his outward protruding belly button. "This was my first clue." He forced a sad smile and lowered his shirt. "I never asked if I could do it because I was afraid of what the guys would say. Understand?"

I could see myself standing alone in the center of the wrestling gym. Sure I understood. I put my arm around Eugene's shoulder. With my free hand I pulled up my shirt and pointed to my belly button. "I've been a lifelong member too. How would you like to join a new exclusive club? It's called the O.A.C."

"O.A.C. ? What does that stand for?"

"Outie Athletic Club. I got the training schedule from Dan yesterday. He uses it to get the wrestlers in shape. If we follow this, in twelve weeks you and I should be in great shape."

"When do we start?" asked Eugene.

"Tomorrow!"

"I'm in!" said Eugene, slapping my palm.

"No, you're out and so am I!"

CHAPTER
SIXTEEN

After it was all over I wished someone had taken videos of our training. Then I could have gone back and put together a highlights film with music and captions and special effects. I know exactly how I'd want it to be. All the titles would be in big bold red letters.

W E SQUARED PRODUCTIONS
in association with
CINEKYD ENTERPRISES
PRESENTS
The Dewimping of Eugenes

WEEK ONE

(The camera would fade into a scene from the first day.)

"Read that again," said Eugene. "That can't be right."

I checked the paper again. "It says here, lie on your back on the floor. Grab the bar with both hands and lift it up above your chest ten times. Rest. Start with sets of ten."

"Not that part," said Eugene. "The part that says begin with sixty pounds. That sounds like too much weight to start with."

"Here it is," I said, pointing with my index finger to the number sixty. "If you think sixty pounds is too much to start with, I'll show you how it's done."

"Okay, Arnold SchwarzenRamboEastwood, go to it," he replied.

"Okay, let me lie down on my back like this. Now you hand me the bar." Eugene grabbed the bar and slowly lowered it into my hands.

"Have it?"

"Yeeeeeeh. Now stand over me, and if I tell you it's getting too heavy, grab it quick. Now up one . . . whew . . . down. Up two . . . whew . . . down . . . up three . . . whew down . . . uuuuuuuup four . . . whew down. Uuuuuuuuup fffffiiiiivvve, it's slipping, Eugene, help grab it!" He grabbed, I pushed, it slipped, I ducked. Smash! Crash!

"You can uncover your face now," said Eugene. "It missed your head by a good inch and a half."

I felt my head to see if everything was in its proper place and I wasn't bleeding. "Everything's okay. Nothing's broken."

"Yes, there is," he replied.

I checked my face again. "I can't find anything broken."

"Look!" insisted Eugene.

I sat up. There beside me was a large crater in the sidewalk. "What are we going to do?"

"Get fit by lugging around sixty-pound bags of cement!"

WEEK TWO

"Eight, nine, ten, eleven . . ." I can't believe I have nine more push-ups to do. "Twelve, whew . . . thirteen . . . whew . . . four—"

"Hi." I looked up and saw Mr. Roberts looking down at me struggling on the floor. "What's this all about?"

"—teen. I thought whew . . . fifteen . . . I would . . . sixteen . . . whew . . . work . . . seventeen . . . out . . . whew . . . whew . . . eighteen . . . a nine- teeeeeeen . . . whew whew whew . . . a little . . . twenty." I collapsed in a heap on the floor, trying to catch my breath.

"When did you start doing this?" he asked.

"A couple weeks ago while you were—" I paused and reluctantly finished my sentence. "Away." I stood up and began to touch my toes so I didn't have to look at him. "I was doing some work here on Saturday and one of the staff, I forget who, said you were out of town. Where did you go?"

He smiled. "I went to the Coast for a quick visit with my son."

We were now face-to-face. "Did you have a nice time?" Mr. Roberts nodded. "I took your advice and wrote to my father. He never wrote back."

"How long ago did you write?"

"Way back in December. I guess he's busy with work."

"Busy or not, I think I'd be a little angry if I hadn't gotten a reply by now."

"Naw, I'm sure he'll write. Listen, I have to go. Catch you later."

WEEK THREE

I hadn't been looking for anything special when I got the mail today but there it was, the same double-wrapped brown package I had sent out more than two months ago. Across the address was stamped in smudged black letters

RETURN TO SENDER
ADDRESSEE UNKNOWN

Without warning, my eyes filled with tears. "That stupid mailman. Doesn't he know who's on his route?" I heaved the tape into the air as high as I could, but caught it just before it hit the ground.

I stomped into the garage and got my good aluminum bat. I tossed the tape up about head high and waited for it to descend into the strike zone. Then I unleashed a picture-perfect swing that split the wrapping, splintered the plastic, and sent the mutilated tape flying in all directions. "I hate you, you jerk! I never want to see you ever again!" I yelled as loud as I could over and over, still swinging the bat continuously in every direction. I don't know how long I kept that up, but when I finally finished my arms ached and I was out of breath. I looked around to see if anyone had seen my outburst. There was no one in sight. I wiped all the remaining signs of my unhappiness away with my sleeve and walked calmly inside with the rest of the mail.

"Hi, Mom. My day was great. How was yours?"

WEEK FOUR

"Are you sure this is part of the training?" asked Eugene.

"I'm positive," I replied as I ate another mouthful. "I need to gain weight, so I have to be on the spaghetti diet."

"You're lucky."

"You may think I'm lucky, but I have to eat spaghetti three times a day. Did you ever have pancakes and spaghetti for breakfast? How about peanut butter and spaghetti on a bagel for lunch? Yogurt and spaghetti for a snack."

Eugene looked green. "What diet should I be on?" he asked.

"You should be on the seafood diet."

"I love seafood."

"No," I replied. *"See food!* All you can do is look. No eating allowed."

WEEK SIX

"Mom, do I look bigger?"

"You mean taller?" she asked as she looked me over.

"No, bigger. My muscles, do they look a little bigger?"

She walked around me three times before she answered. "Yeah . . . maybe a little."

"Can you really see it?"

"I think so," she replied.

"You're not lying to me, are you?"

"No. Your arms do look a little bigger."

I lifted up my shirt. "What about my chest?"

"Maybe a little."

"Really?"

"Yes."

"Really?"

"Yes!"

I'm not sure she really saw any difference, but I'll accept the fib. "Thanks, Mom."

WEEK SEVEN

"Do you think both of us should be hanging on this branch at the same time?" asked Eugene.

"How can we see who reaches thirty chin-ups first if we both don't do it at the same time?"

"I know that, but this branch doesn't look strong enough!"

"You know something, Eugene?" I said. "You're always worried that something's going to go wrong. This branch is so thick that four people could hang on it at the same time and nothing would happen. Now are you ready to lose this contest?"

"A pizza to the winner," he replied.

"You're on. Ready." Both of us hung down from the limb. "Set . . . everybody keeps his own count . . . go."

"One . . . one, two . . . two, three . . . three, four . . . four, ten . . . ten, six . . . *crack* . . . siiiiiiix . . . *splash.*

"Gene? Are you all right?"

"I think so," I replied, checking to see that everything was still attached. "How about you?"

"Yeah, I'm okay. Can I ask you a very important question?" I nodded. "Do you remember seeing a giant mud puddle under this limb when we climbed this tree?"

WEEK EIGHT

I stood in front of the mirror bare-chested and flexed my arms upward. My arms definitely looked bigger. Next, I posed like a gorilla and studied my chest from all angles. There was no question about it. My weeks of work were paying off. This time my mother wouldn't have to lie.

WEEK ELEVEN

"Are you sure this is right?"

"We've been doing this for eight weeks now and you still don't trust me. Do you?"

"It's not that," said Eugene. "It's just that I didn't see this exercise at all on the yellow sheet and I just wonder where you got this."

"Dan gave me some other sheets about a week ago and this was on one of them." I took the crumpled sheet out of my pocket. "Look here."

"You're right," said Eugene. "That's what it says. It's just that, well, ah . . . don't you feel a little funny walking around the neighborhood with a knapsack full of rocks strapped to your back?"

"Will you stop worrying so much? People don't know you're carrying rocks. Besides, walking on flat ground is just the beginning. We have to find a hill and run up it a couple of times."

"A hill? Can't we take a break for lunch?"

"We just had lunch."

"But that was an hour ago. How about a little snack?"

"And ruin your diet? Look!" I said, pointing to a rise just beyond some tall bushes. "That hill's perfect."

"But the sign over there says

Private Property, No Trespassing."

"There you go again. Worrying for nothing. Running up a hill a couple times to train and trespassing are different in my book. Let's cut in here through these bushes." I jogged into the open field toward the bottom of the hill.

"I don't like this." Eugene scowled, pausing at the bushes to look around. "Wait up a minute, you're running too fast." I stopped at the bottom of the hill to let him catch up and then we both continued up the hill.

"This is supposed to build up all the muscles in your body. I can really feel it in my back."

"Hey," cried Eugene from behind me. "Don't these grounds look familiar?"

"Not to me. This is the first time I've ever been over in this neighborhood."

"Something's very familiar about this place," whined Eugene. "Wait. Do you hear that?"

"I didn't hear anything," I replied. "Listen, if you just don't want to do this exercise, then say so, stop, but don't pull that 'Hey, what's that noise' routine on me."

"No, really. I'm not kidding. Is that barking?"

"Hearing barking noises? Hmm . . . And how long have you—" From out of nowhere two large black barking

Dobermans appeared, heading straight up the hill for Eugene and me.

I yelled out, *"It's Tiny and Walter! Run!"*

"What'll we do?" yelled Eugene. "We'll never outrun them!"

"I know!" I replied. "The only one I have to outrun is you."

We both made it up to the top of the hill safely. You never know how fast you can run until a Doberman challenges you to a race.

WEEK TWELVE

Wendy and Andi walked around Eugene and me, pausing occasionally to whisper to each other.

"How much weight have you lost, Eugene?" asked Wendy.

"Twelve pounds," he replied, beaming with pride.

She gave him a big hug and an equally big kiss. "You look terrific!"

I looked over at Andi, hoping she would say something complimentary too. "Bet you could whip that jerk in school now if you wanted too."

"Think so?"

"I know so." She opened her arms, I think to hug me, too, but I grabbed her left hand and shook it. "Thanks. Thanks a lot." I didn't stay around to find out if anything else would follow the handshake.

CHAPTER
SEVENTEEN

Tryout day finally arrived. The audion was dark except for the spotlight that lit up the audition area in the front.

"You're next," said Mr. Roberts, pointing to me as soon as I walked in the door.

"I'm not ready yet," I replied.

"The auditions will be over in ten minutes. It's now or never."

How can that be? I thought. I just got here. "I thought auditions went on all day."

Mr. Roberts puffed harder and faster on his pipe. A thick cloud of smoke was beginning to circle his face so you almost couldn't see him. "Well, are you coming up here or not?"

Confused and getting more nervous by the minute, I slowly walked to the front of the room and sat down in a hard wooden chair. The lights seemed hotter than I remembered. "See that yellow sheet in front of you?" There were three yellow sheets, so I grabbed the nearest one and held it up. "There are three passages on that paper. Pick one out and read it to me. Ready?" The cameramen nodded their heads. "Five . . . four . . . three . . . two . . . and roll 'em."

Things were happening a little too fast for me. I scanned the first paragraph, but it didn't make any sense. I thought, Boy, this is really Greek to me, when I realized the first passage was really written in Greek. The second passage wasn't much better. It was in Japanese, and the third, I think was in Hebrew. "I can't read these," I replied as I saw my hopes for a part slowly go down the drain.

"You're trying out for Simba, aren't you?" I nodded. "Then it doesn't matter if you can't read them, because Simba doesn't have much of a speaking part." Mr. Roberts got up from his chair and walked over to a door on the left side of the room. He opened it and calmly said, "All you have to do to get the part is wrestle this Bengal tiger and beat him."

"A Bengal tiger? Ha-ha-ha-ha. *A Bengal tiger."* That Mr. Roberts really cracks me up sometimes.

"What's so funny?" he asked.

I was laughing so hard, it was difficult to get the words out. "I thought you said wrestle a Bengal tiger."

"I did," he replied. There in the doorway stood the biggest Bengal tiger I had ever seen. The minute the cat spotted me, he smiled, if that's possible, and without warning leapt. The weight of his body knocked me backward off the chair and I landed on my floor, tangled in my covers, clutching my pillow. I looked up at the clock. It was 4:30 A.M. I sat on the side of my bed repeating, "It was only a nightmare. It was only a nightmare," until I finally fell asleep again. The real audition couldn't be worse.

Wendy and Eugene were waiting for me in the back of the auditioning studio when I arrived at Cinekyd the next morning.

"Nervous?" asked Wendy.

"Nervous?" I repeated, with a laugh. "Me? Nervous? I just wrestled a Bengal tiger. Why should I be nervous?"

"You did what with who?" asked Eugene.

"You had to be there," I replied. "Listen, Eugene, there's something important I have to tell you." I took a very deep breath and swallowed hard three times. "You know that fitness magazine?"

"I know."

"That fitness test that I gave you—"

"I know."

"It wasn't really in the magazine."

"I know."

"I made it up."

"I know."

"I know it wasn't the right thing to do but—"

"I know."

"But I wasn't sure . . . you know?" Eugene nodded. "How?"

"I get that magazine."

"Then why didn't you say something?"

"I wanted to see how far you were going to go with it and when I saw you wanted someone to work out with you, I figured why not."

"Then you're not mad?"

Eugene put his arm around me. "Mad 'cause you helped me lose twelve pounds? Are you kidding!"

"Who's next?" asked Mr. Roberts.

I stood up and confidently replied, "I'll go."

"Very brave," said Wendy kiddingly as she gave me the thumbs-up sign.

"Brave, maybe," countered Eugene. "I think he just wants to get it over with. Hey, good luck."

I handed my registration form to Mr. Roberts and sat down on a comfortable sofa at the front of the room. I could see Mr. Roberts clearly, but beyond him the room looked black.

"Okay, just relax. Pretend we're just having a conversation. Cameras ready?" I saw the cameramen nod their heads. "Decks rolling. Five . . . four . . . three . . . two . . . one . . . Tell me your name."

"Eugene Lockheart."

"Where do you go to school, Gene?"

"Cherrydale Junior High."

"Do you like school?"

"Sometimes."

"When?"

"When we have science, and math."

"I see from your application that you're going to continue with still photography this summer and try a little acting too." I nodded. "What got you interested in acting?"

"You did." Mr. Roberts smiled. "Remember Professor Doctor Professor?"

"How could vee forget? Ready for today?" I nodded. "In front of you is a piece of paper with three paragraphs on it. Pick one and read it."

I scanned the paper and breathed a sigh of relief. All three selections were written in English. "I think I'll read selection number two." I cleared my throat two times and began.

Wait a minute. What was that? Everybody stop and don't move.

I paused and looked off to the side, and then ducked my head as if to avoid something.

There it is again. Do you hear it? It sounds like a giant insect!

I ducked my head again and swatted the air in front of me.

Look, we're being attacked by poisonous flying insects. A bite by one of these is fatal since there is no antidote. The only thing we have to kill them with is bare hands. Be careful not to get scratched by the stinger.

I calmly put the paper down on the table and slowly, with calculated cunning, raised my hands and clapped them together in front of my eyes.

"Cut!" said Mr. Roberts. "That was great. You made the actions look great."

I smiled as I picked up a small black speck from the table in front of me. When I reached the table where Mr. Roberts was sitting, I paused. "I cannot tell a lie. I had outside help with my part today. Open your hand." Puzzled, Mr. Roberts opened his left hand. Without breaking stride I dropped a wasp into it, and not waiting for an answer, proceeded back to my chair.

"Well, how'd I do?"

"Great!" said Eugene.

"A winner," said Wendy, smiling. I looked back at Andi, who was on camera one. She flashed me a giant smile. Now it was up to Roberts and the staff to decide.

CHAPTER
EIGHTEEN

That night I was sure I had gotten the part of Simba. But as the week dragged on, I wasn't so certain. By Friday I was a mess.

"Hey! Don't you say hello?"

"Huh?"

"Earth to Eugene! Earth to Eugene! Come in, Eugene."

"Huh?" Andi slammed her math book into the locker beside her. "Oh! Andi! Hi. What's up?"

"Nice of you to establish contact with the intelligent life on this planet."

"Sorry." My cheeks felt hot. "I guess I wasn't paying much attention."

"Tomorrow's the big day," said Andi.

"Huh? Tomorrow's Saturday."

"You're not too nervous, are you?"

"Huh? Nervous?" Now my forehead felt hot. "I guess

I'm really out of it today." Come to think of it, every time I see Andi I'm out of it.

Andi started to laugh. "That's exactly how I was last year."

It was good to hear that. "You were this bad?"

"Pretty close. Your fog may be a little thicker."

"Huh?" I replied. This time I was joking.

Then, without warning, she took a small step toward me. "I have a feeling that you're going to get the part of Simba tomorrow."

"You do?" . . . There I was standing on the limb of a giant tree in the deepest, darkest part of the jungle. On another limb about two hundred yards away a massive boa constrictor was squeezing the life out of Andi. I beat my chest and let out a glass-shattering yell. *"Oweeehhhaahhh-hoahweeehhhaaahh."* That was jungle for "It's curtains for you, snake." I grabbed a thick green vine marked north–south expressway and swung over. With one hand behind my back I squish-smashed the snake, sending it to snake purgatory. Andi threw her arms around me and gave me a long, juicy kiss. *"Me Simba, you Andi,"* I yelled as I grabbed the Vine Street extension and headed home. . . .

Then the bell for sixth period rang. "I've got to go. We have a test in English." I leaned against the locker and stared. Halfway down the hall Andi turned and yelled, "Good luck. I'll see you at Cinekyd tomorrow."

I stood in the hall long after it had emptied. The smile was still on my face when I walked in late to math class.

After school I couldn't wait to get home and call Eugene. There was no answer. I tried again every half hour until his mother finally answered at six-fifteen.

"Mrs. Risen, is Eugene there?"

"Why, no," she replied. "He's at Cinekyd."

"Have him call me as soon as he gets in."

"I will. Nice talking to you."

I hung up the phone and flopped down on the sofa in the den. Hardly anyone goes to Cinekyd after school on Fridays. What's he doing there? I'll bet he's trying to find out if he got a part. That's just like him.

When I hadn't heard from him by nine, I was sorry I hadn't called him back earlier. When he hadn't called by ten, I was just plain mad and that's how I went to bed.

I got up at eleven the next morning. "Eugene called while you were sleeping," yelled my mother from downstairs. "He asked me if you could meet him for lunch today at the pizza place near Cinekyd. I told him you'd call him when you got up, but he had to go out with his mom so I said okay for you. It was okay, wasn't it?"

"Sure," I yelled back.

"You'll have just enough time to get ready."

Eugene was standing at the counter waiting for me. "Steak sandwich for me, and you?"

"Spaghetti."

"Let's sit over there," he said, pointing to a booth.

Eugene sat down. "This is going to be the best summer of our lives."

"We'll know soon," I replied. "How come you didn't call me back last night?"

"I got home around ten and my mom thought it was too late to call."

"Where were you so late?"

"I was at Cinekyd."

I looked Eugene squarely in the eye. "You were? What were you doing there so late?"

"I stopped in after school to finish up a little editing, and

111

Mr. Roberts asked me if I wanted to stay for dinner and watch a movie. So I did."

"Really? What does his place look like?"

"What's the matter, don't you believe me?"

"Come on, what does it look like?"

"Number six!" yelled a girl behind the counter. We walked over in silence and got our food. As soon as we sat down I looked at Eugene and repeated, "Well, what does it look like? Huh?"

Eugene cleared his throat three times. Maybe now he would learn to tell the truth. "We ate in a room that looked like a combination den and eating area. There were three doors. One led to a bathroom, the other one—"

"You were there last night." I smashed my fist against the table so hard, my dish rattled.

"I told you I was." A smug smile signaled his victory. "In case you haven't noticed it, I haven't lied to you, or anybody for that matter, for months. I've changed."

"What did you do up there?" I asked, ignoring his comment.

"We had spaghetti and we watched an old John Wayne war movie. You should have seen it. John Wayne and his men were surrounded by—"

"Listen, Eugene, we've got to over to Cinekyd soon, so why don't you eat your lunch? You can tell me about the movie some other time."

Eugene wrinkled his nose, bobbed his head back and forth, and in a singsong voice replied, "I thought you were interested in what happened last night."

"You don't have to tell me every little detail!" I snapped.

"Excuse *me*!" said Eugene. "Maybe if you stopped worrying whether I'm telling the truth and paid more attention to how you're always feeling sorry for yourself, you'd be a lot better off. Look at yourself in the mirror sometimes. *Peewee.*"

"You're full of it, *Tubby.*" He's just saying that because I said he was a liar.

"Ask Wendy or Andi if you don't believe me, *Shorty.* They'll tell you."

I dug my fork into my spaghetti, and with grace and skill flung it in his direction. The spaghetti hit him squarely in the nose, slid down his cheeks and onto his pants. "Is that so, *Fatso?*"

He took his napkin and wiped his face. Then he stood up and leaned across the table and grabbed a handful of spaghetti. We were chin-to-chin like, and then Eugene dumped the whole handful on my head. *"Shrimp."* It slid off the sides and caught on my ears.

I grabbed a fistful with my left and stretched the neck of his T-shirt and dropped it in. I smiled as I mashed the lump with both hands. *"Tubby."*

Eugene grabbed the catsup and squirted it. It left a modern design on my shirt. "Catsup on your spaghetti, *Twerp!*"

I grabbed the mustard and covered the back of both his hands. "Mustard on your steak, *Porker!*"

We stared at each other for a long time without saying anything. Finally, Eugene got up to go. "Oh, by the way, I snuck a look at the list to see who got a part. You got Simba. Some Simba you'll be." He shook his head, grabbed a handful of napkins, and started to go. Halfway across the restaurant he stopped and yelled, "Like it or not, I got the part of Bart Adam." And he left.

I sat alone in the booth for a long time. So Roberts has everybody up for dinner. I don't care. Then I thought about my father. We were sitting at the kitchen table two years ago on Valentine's Day. "How's my special guy?" he asked.

I gritted my teeth and stared into my empty cereal bowl. "Okay."

Dad got up and came over to my chair. Placing his arm around me he said, "I know I promised to take you to the ballgame, but what can I do?"

"Nothing," I replied.

"I'll make it up to you. I promise."

If I'm your special guy how come everything else comes first? I thought to myself but I couldn't ask. "I know."

"That's my guy."

I wiped the tears from my eyes with my sleeve. "That's right," I said out loud to an imaginary pipe-smoking man in front of me. "Invite me up for dinner, tell me I should try out for a part in the movie, make me think that I'm something special to you and . . ." I paused to grit my teeth. "And then do the exact same thing with Eugene and Wendy and everyone else in the place. First my father lets me down, and then you. Well, you may have fooled me once, Mr. Roberts, but it's never going to happen to this guy again. If you think that means I'm giving up my part in the movie and quitting again, you're wrong. You can't get rid of me that easily. It just means . . . well, you'll see.

"And as for you, Big Mouth *Tuns of Fun* Eugene . . ." The tears were starting again. "You're wrong. I am very happy!"

"Hey, you going to clean up this mess?" The girl with the apron was standing by the booth, hands folded. She dropped a wet rag on the table.

"Don't worry," I said as I grabbed the rag. Inside I knew that the other mess would be much harder to clean up.

CHAPTER
NINETEEN

For the next week and a half I stayed away from Cinekyd.

Ring. "Andi's on the phone for you," said Mom.

"Tell her I'll call her later."

Ring. "It's Wendy."

"Take a message."

Ring. "Eugene wants to know if you'll be at Cinekyd tomorrow."

"Tell him I can't."

Mom held up the phone, pointed to me, and mouthed, "You tell him." I shook my head no and went into the den. She joined me a minute later. "Is there something wrong?" I shook my head no. "Did something happen at Cinekyd?" Another no. "You haven't been there for a week."

"I was too busy to go."

"You sat around and did your hide-in-front-of-the-TV bit."

"I did not!" I snapped. Now I could add Mom to the list of people who hated me. Mom reached over and squeezed my knee before disappearing into the kitchen. I picked up the phone and started to dial Eugene's house. Just before I got to the last number, I hung up. Now was not the right time to talk. I dug my fist into the pillow beside me. Maybe there never would be a right time.

I overslept the first morning of the summer program. Slightly out of breath I slipped quietly into a seat on the back row, hoping my late arrival would go unnoticed.

"Good morning, Eugene," bellowed Mr. Roberts. I forced a smile as everyone turned around to look. "What does it mean if the big hand is on the five and the little hand is on the nine?" Everyone started to snicker.

I wasn't going to let him get the best of me again. I stood up and folded my arms across my chest. I made sure my face was expressionless. "It means it's five minutes after nine."

"Very good," he replied sarcastically. "So that means you're five minutes late and . . ." He started to walk down the center aisle toward me, but he stopped a few rows short. I could have passed for a statue in the park. "That puts us all five minutes behind schedule. We only have six weeks to shoot this movie. A minute here and a minute there mounts up. Nine o'clock means nine o'clock. Understand?" There was dead silence.

I watched him go back to the podium. "Now where was I?" I smirked as I slowly sat down. The pressing angry tone still present in his voice meant nothing to me now. "I want Eugene, Wendy, and Eugene up front now immediately. The rest of you go with your crews but make sure you're back here when it's time to practice your scene."

I planned to settle things with Eugene before rehearsal began. As I started down the aisle toward him, he was coming up toward me. "Where you been, stranger?" he asked. I saw no signs that he was still mad.

"At home." I took a long, deep breath and forced a half smile. The apology speech had been rehearsed a million times. "Eugene . . ." My throat was so dry, I could hardly swallow. "Eugene . . ." I began again. "We'd better get down front or we'll be late for rehearsal." Maybe later.

As we sat down Mr. Roberts walked over to a giant pad of paper resting on an easel next to the podium. On it he wrote:

LEVEL ONE—LEARN

LEVEL TWO—HIT

LEVEL THREE—BECOME

"Your goal this summer," he said, looking each of us square in the eye and then pointing to what he had just written on the pad, "is first to *learn* your lines and your marks. That's level one."

"What's a mark?" asked Eugene.

"Sorry, I forgot some of you are new at this. A mark is, where you walk to or where you stand in a scene." Roberts paused for questions. I had to force myself to look at him. "In level two, you'll *say* your lines and *hit* your marks. That means, be where you're supposed to be on the set." Mr. Roberts pointed at each of us again. "Ninety-five percent of you will stop at this level. A few select people will achieve level three. That's where you actually *become your character.* You *act, think, feel,* and *behave* exactly like your character would. Since there is no script, I will tell you everything you need to know about what your character does in the scene. Then we'll do it. Ready?"

This ought to be a real trip, I thought. A whole movie without a script.

"We'll start with scene forty-two . . . Okay, now, Eugene, watch what I do." Mr. Roberts lay down on the floor and closed his eyes as if he were asleep. His eyes suddenly flew open and darted from side to side. "Where am I," he shouted as he propped himself up on his elbows. "Get the idea, Eugene?" he asked as he stood up. "You're scared. You don't know where you are. That's what you have to show."

"Now, Wendy, I want you to get up very slowly, like you do in the morning when your mother wakes you up to go to school. You're exhausted, scared, and—

"Gene, you come over here"—he pointed to the center of the set—"and crouch down. Remember you're half boy and half monkey. Pretend you're rubbing sticks together to make a fire, and when you see the two of them open their eyes . . ."

It was amazing to watch Mr. Roberts play each role. But I already knew he was a good actor. Hadn't he acted like he cared? Hadn't he seemed to understand how I felt about my father's leaving?

"Places, everyone. Now you try it!"

Eugene and Wendy lay down on the floor and propped themselves up on their elbows. I pretended to make a fire. Eugene cleared his throat and in a monotone said, "Where am I? Hi, I'm Bart Adams and this is my friend, Professor Hobson."

Mr. Roberts took out his pipe and shook it wildly, sending ashes flying in all directions. "You sound about as scared and worried about what's happening to you as . . . as the weatherman does when he says the forecast for the weekend is hot and sunny. It isn't every day you wake up dripping wet on the bank of a river and see a strange being building a fire. Again! This time with feeling."

"Where am I? . . . . Professor, get up . . . . looook . . . Hi, my name is Bart Adams and this is my friend Professor Hobson. . . . Friends?"

"Better. Again!"

"Where am . . ."

"Again!

"Stop being Eugene and become Simba.

"Almost perfect, again.

"Once more!

"Again!

"We're taping this one. Deck A is rolling. From the top. Five, four, three, two . . . That's a take. Now look at yourselves on the monitor and tell me what you think. I need the people in scene thirty-nine in here right now."

In less than two minutes the tape was over. It looked pretty good, but, one hour's preparation for just two minutes of tape. And this tape was just for us to review, in preparation for the final shooting which would take place later that week, outside, in costume and makeup, under the direction of . . . This was going to be a long six weeks.

CHAPTER
TWENTY

I was putting on my makeup when Eugene appeared at the door. He was already made up and in costume. "You're wearing just a bathing suit?" I nodded. "Do you have another one for formal occasions?"

I forced a laugh. How much longer could we both pretend that nothing had happened between us. "The boss is a real slave driver, isn't he?"

"I heard he's like this every summer. In fact, this summer some people are worried because they say he's acting too nice."

I just shook my head. He's nice, all right. Does a nice person growl at someone he likes? Does a nice person lead someone on and then let him down? That's what I wanted to say then but didn't. Time would come when I would.

"How much time till they shoot our scene?" asked Eugene.

I took the schedule out of the back of my suit and checked. "Three-thirty. That's in thirty minutes." When I finished putting my makeup on, I walked around the room in circles as I went over my lines. Eugene began to whistle something off tune. "Wanna take a walk around the block to kill some time?" I asked. Part of me wanted him to say yes and another, no.

"Sure," he replied.

The walk began in silence. Every time I turned to talk to him, he was looking away. Whenever he turned to look at me, I stared at the ground. I had to really force myself to begin. "So, having a good summer so far?"

"Pretty good. How about you?"

"Okay, I guess." I took a deep breath and looked Eugene straight in the eye. "I'm sorry I called you a liar."

"Forget it, I—"

"Let me finish. I had a lot of time to think about things this past week, and you were right. I've been walking around here and everywhere looking like I'd been sucking on lemons. And I've acted like a real jerk too. How'd you manage to put up with me for this long?"

Eugene chuckled. "It wasn't easy." He grinned and put his arm around me. "You're the first true friend I've ever had. And you're allowed to have your share of bad days. I certainly have mine."

I smiled too. His grin blossomed into a broad smile. We squeezed each other's hand until they both started to change colors. "You did look pretty funny covered in spaghetti."

"Mustard matched your shirt perfectly!"

"Eugene!" Wendy was running toward us at top speed, waving her hands in the air. "Where have you guys been? You're ten minutes late for the shooting."

121

I checked my watch. "It's only three-ten. Our scene is not supposed to be shot for another twenty minutes."

"I don't know what schedule you looked at," she replied, "but our scene goes off at three."

"Look here," I said, taking the schedule out again and showing it to Wendy. "It says it right here—Scene Forty-two . . . shooting time . . . oh, no, three o'clock. I thought it said three-thirty."

We all broke into a run. We made it back to the parking lot in record time. I could see Mr. Roberts banging his pipe against the trunk of a tree. He probably would have enjoyed doing it to our heads.

Since the best offense is a good defense, I walked right up to him and said, "It's my fault Wendy and Eugene are late." Roberts glared at me. I could feel his eyes burning a hole in my forehead. "I misread the schedule."

His index finger stopped inches from my nose. "Everything's fifteen minutes behind now because of *you!*" he growled.

I wanted to yell "So what," but instead my reply could hardly be heard. "I know."

Roberts glared at me for a second and then stamped away. "All right," he roared. "Show's over. Let's get to work."

I kicked the dirt with my bare foot so hard I cracked the nail on my big toe. If a Bengal tiger came out of the bushes right now, I'll bet I could take him. When Roberts walked past me again, I made a fist but hid it behind my back. "Places, everyone." I walked to the campfire site and crouched down. I opened my hand. "Camera's ready."

"Ready."

"Decks rolling."

"Decks A and B are rolling," said Andi.

"Five, four, three, two . . ."

Eugene propped himself up on his elbows and paused. "Where am I? What's going to happen now?" The scene went off without a flaw.

"Cut! That's a take. Simba, I want you to look a little more like you're scared this time. Okay, everybody, we're doing the scene again, only this time in closeup. Sound people, move the equipment in low and very tight. All pictures this time will be from the waist up. Ready, roll 'em."

"Hi, I'm Bart Adams and this is my assistant, Professor Hobson. Thanks for saving our lives." I looked over at Eugene.

"Cut! Simba, Eugene, whatever your name is. You're supposed to look surprised and afraid, not like you just got up. Understand?" I nodded. "Start again. Five . . . four . . . three . . . two . . ."

"Thanks for saving our lives." I opened my mouth and pulled my body backward.

"Cut. Simba, your mouth is open like you're at the dentist. But you still don't look scared."

I gritted my teeth. Why was he getting on my back like this?

"Here, let me show you how." Mr. Roberts opened his mouth slightly and widened his eyes.

That's how I just looked. What does he want from me anyway?

"Let's go again from the top. Five . . . four . . . three . . . two . . ."

"Thanks for saving our lives." I opened my mouth slowly and widened my eyes, copying Mr. Roberts's example exactly.

"Cut! Now you're turning your head away from the camera. What's the matter with you today? Can't you do anything right?"

My muscles tightened again and I made two fists.

"Try and do it right this time." I felt like I was going to explode. "Cameras rolling." My face felt like it was on fire. "Five . . . four . . ." I stood up and glared at Mr. Roberts. "Three . . . two . . ." I dropped the sticks into the fireplace and started to walk away from the set. "Gene, where are you going?" I didn't bother to turn around. That guy may get away with pushing other kids around, but not me. "Gene, wait!" As far as I was concerned, that guy and this place were history.

CHAPTER
TWENTY-ONE

Mr. Roberts caught up with me just as I left the parking lot. He grabbed my arm, but I jerked it free and kept walking. "Wait, I want to talk to you." I kept walking. "Will you wait for a second?"

Without turning around I yelled as loud as I could, "You can't tell me what to do!"

His reply was equally loud. "You're telling me that the director can't tell his actors what to do?"

I turned around but continued to walk backward. "No, I mean yes, I mean that's different."

Mr. Roberts stopped. He folded his hands and watched me continue my retreat. "I'm not going to run after you anymore." My pace slowed and I took smaller steps. Roberts took his fist and pounded it into his thigh. "Will you stop being so pigheaded and just stand still for a second?"

Part of me said keep walking while the other part said

stop and listen. "Okay," I said, pausing for a moment. "Say what you have to say."

"Why did you run away like that?" he asked.

"Why were you picking on me like that?"

Mr. Roberts shook his head. "Picking on you? I wasn't picking on you. I was just trying to get you to do better."

"Call it what you like," I replied. "It was picking to me." Mr. Roberts unfolded his arms. He searched his left pocket for his pipe and methodically refilled it with tobacco. I put my hands on my hips and tapped my bare foot rhythmically on the ground. "Is there anything else you want to say?"

"As a matter of fact, there is." Roberts paused to light his pipe. "Is there something wrong?"

Now it was my turn to fold my hands. "Nope."

"I don't mean just now. I mean for the past few weeks."

"Nope."

Mr. Roberts looked at me intently. "Then why have you purposely tried to avoid me?"

I almost started to walk away again. "I don't know what you're talking about."

"First you disappear from here for a week and a half and when you reappear, you take off in the other direction every time you see me."

"I did not!" I replied adamantly.

"You haven't come to my office to show me the pictures you've taken . . ."

"I've been very busy."

". . . or even just to talk."

"What's more important, talking to you or getting my work done?"

Mr. Roberts took a step toward me and I responded by taking a step backward. "You want *me* to believe that in this past week there hasn't been thirty seconds for you to stop in and say hello?"

"That's right!" I knew my answer was dumb, but I said it anyway.

"Come on, now. You can't be serious. There's got to be something else."

"Maybe I wasn't cut out to be an actor."

"You were cut out to be an actor when you tried out for the part," he replied. "What's happened?"

"Maybe the tryout was an accident." Now I was feeling sorry for myself.

"Maybe it was," said Mr. Roberts, parroting my tone. "But I don't think so."

He was starting to sweet-talk me again and I didn't like it. "Listen, you leave me alone and I'll leave you alone and everything will be just fine. You got plenty of kids to invite up for spaghetti. I don't need you anymore." My face flushed and my heart felt like it was going to leap out of my chest.

Mr. Roberts shook his head in dismay. "What are you talking about?"

"I don't like to be led on. That's what. Understand?"

"Led on? How does having you up for dinner lead you on?"

I took a deep breath and stared at the cement sidewalk. "When you had me over for dinner that night in the beginning of the year I felt"—the lump in my throat was getting bigger—"like I was worth something. Then you helped me fill in for Dave in the *Dusty's Clubhouse* episode. And you kept on telling me how I should try out for the summer movie. You know my father hardly had time to do anything with me. You couldn't do enough. Want to know how dumb I was? Huh? Listen to this. I thought you were doing this just for me. Can you believe that? I really thought I was special." I wiped the wetness out of both eyes with my sleeves. "Then I found out you invite *everyone* up for dinner."

Mr. Roberts smiled confidently and began to approach me again. "You are special. Everyone here at Cinekyd is special in their own way."

I kept shaking my head no. "Sure . . . And what movie did you get that phony line from?"

Mr. Roberts pointed his finger at me. "Listen, I meant what I just said."

"That's what my fa—" Uncontrollable tears were rolling down my cheeks. "My father always told me how important I was too. And now he won't even answer my letters." I hid my face and tried futilely to stop crying. "I can't depend on anybody!"

The next thing I felt was two big strong arms wrapping themselves around my shoulders and steadying me. My arms were limp at first but they slowly found their way around Mr. Roberts's waist, and I squeezed back.

We hugged in silence for a long time. I was the first one to let go. "My makeup's all messed up."

Mr. Roberts took the sleeve of his shirt and wiped both my cheeks. "You have to learn to depend on yourself now."

I put my arm around Mr. Roberts and together we walked back to the set. I didn't say a word to anyone until after we finished filming our scene.

"What happened?" asked Eugene, Wendy, and Andi all at once.

"Mr. Roberts yelled at me for walking off and I yelled back at him for yelling at me."

"You should have seen the look he had on his face when

he went after you," said Wendy. "I thought he was going to kill you."

"Me too," said Andi. "He looked vicious."

"Tiny and Walter are vicious," I replied with a twinkle in my eye. "Mr. Roberts is a pussycat."

CHAPTER
TWENTY-TWO

What Mr. Roberts told me that afternoon didn't change things right away.

"Hey, Gene, what you been doing with yourself?"

"Taking pictures . . . practicing my lines. Nothing much."

"Stop up and say hello sometimes."

"I'm too—" I smiled. "Maybe later on this afternoon."

Sometimes I caught myself running out to the mailbox hoping to find a letter. But as the summer wore on I gradually thought less of my father and a little more of Mr. Roberts.

That didn't mean that things were peaceful at Cinekyd, because they weren't. On the set Roberts was as gruff as ever.

"Aren't you ever going to get this right?"

"I did it just like you told me," I shouted back.

"I told you to do it this way, not that way!"

But I wasn't the only one. "No, Wendy, no!"

"Eugene! Will you ever wake up?"

"What kind of a camera angle is that, Andi? The audience will have to tilt their heads to see what's going on."

The four of us met secretly one night to hear a plan I devised to get back at the Boss. Not in a mean way, but in a video way.

"What if he finds out about this?" asked Eugene.

With a straight face I replied, "He'll paint you blue, Wendy red, Andi silver, and me gold and hang us from the small Christmas tree in the back."

"I used to be the right shape to decorate a tree, but not anymore," said Eugene.

"I think we can pull it off," said Wendy.

"Me too," replied Andi.

"Then you're all with me?"

"Yes!" they said.

"We really have our work cut out for us if we want to get it ready in time for the banquet. Here's what I want you to do. Wendy, you . . ."

The final three days of the summer program were always spent staying at some motel and shooting on location. This year we were traveling to a place in the Delaware River called Swamp Island. During the Civil War the North used this island as a munitions dump and prison camp. We were going to use the munitions dump as a jungle temple, the basement corridors of the prison camp for the most elaborate chase scene ever attempted by Cinekyd, and a nearby pond for my daring rescue of Eugene and Wendy.

A noisy five-van caravan left the Cinekyd parking lot at 9:00 A.M. sharp, and two hours later we arrived at our desti-

131

nation. Amid a large, welcoming crowd of enthusiastic townspeople, we unloaded our equipment and began our afternoon's work.

"If this is done right, it'll be the best scene in the film," said Dan, handing Tommy a plastic gun. "Put this in your right hand." Dan placed us face-to-face about a foot apart. "We're going to pick up the scene from just after Tommy says, 'This is the end of the line for you two.' Now, Gene, when you hear that, look quickly to your left as if you see something coming. When Tommy turns to look, you grab the gun hand with your right hand and pull Tommy toward you. As you spin him around slip your body behind him. Now, try it slowly."

"Again, faster!"

"Faster!"

"Great. You're doing great. Now from there I want you to grab the gun with your left hand and knock it away. Then lift Tommy up gently and lay him down on the ground. End the battle by pretending to knock him out. As soon as you're sure he's out, dive into the water and save your friends. Go to it!"

For the next hour and a half Tommy and I practiced and practiced and practiced. "Not bad," said Dan. "I want the two of you to practice this after dinner and I'll meet with you again in the morning for a final runthrough."

By the time the scene was ready to be filmed the next day, Tommy and I could do it in our sleep.

"Scene forty-one," barked Mr. Roberts. "Let's get all the equipment down to that pond. Fast! We're running a little behind."

As everybody moved down to the pond I lingered behind for just a minute. I closed my eyes, gritted my teeth, and banged my fists against my thighs. I repeated my chant silently. *Go get 'em, Simba. You can do it!* I took a deep breath and puffed out my chest. A loud whoop followed and I ran toward the pond. I was ready. I was Simba.

"Let's get going," said Mr. Roberts. "Wendy, Eugene, over here.

"Roll A! *Roll B!*"

"Decks rolling."

"Five . . . four . . . three . . . two . . ."

Fear and panic filled the faces of Eugene and Wendy as Tommy tied them up. Suddenly there was a bloodcurdling yell, and I appeared from the underbrush.

Tommy drew his gun. "Stay where you are or I'll shoot you." I froze, but every time he turned to look at Eugene and Wendy, I inched a little closer. "This is the end of the line for you two," said Tommy with a nasty laugh, and he pushed them into the water. "And as for you . . ."

As Eugene and Wendy screamed and flailed helplessly in the water, I lunged at Tommy, grabbing his right arm with such force that it spun him around and caused the gun to go flying into the air. My heart was racing, and I could feel every hair on my body standing up at attention. With a bloodcurdling yell, I wrapped my left arm around his waist and, in one fluid motion, wrestled him to the ground. I think my fist brushed by his nose when I swung at him, and then he went limp.

I leapt to my feet, grabbed the rubber knife from my belt, and ran toward the water. I put the knife in my mouth just before I dived into the water, and swam furiously toward their motionless bodies. When I reached them, I pretended to cut their ropes and with one in each hand, towed them safely to shore. At first they lay lifeless on the edge of the pond, but soon they began to stir. I pounded my chest and, facing skyward, let out another ear-shattering yell.

"Cut! That's a take!" Everyone was on their feet applauding. Eugene's hand met mine in a high five. Wendy gave me a bear hug. I grabbed Andi and swung her around in a circle. Dizzy and out of breath, the two of us collapsed on the ground.

I didn't stay down for long, though. I spotted a small tree by the pond and climbed up to the first branch. Hanging only by my right arm, I beat my chest with my left and howled *"Ahyee! Ahyee! Ahyee! Ahyee!"* I was swinging around and carrying on so much, I didn't see Mr. Roberts come over and lean against the tree.

"You really have become Simba," said Mr. Roberts, chuckling.

"Oh! Hi." I could feel my face getting red.

"I wanted to come over and tell you what a great job you did."

I held up three fingers. "Was it a level-three performance?" I whooped.

He lit his pipe and shook his head no.

I let go of the branch and landed on the ground. "What do you mean, *no!*" I shouted.

A sly smile crept onto his face as he held up ten fingers. "That, my friend, was a level ten!"

"Thanks. By the way, you better not hang around here much longer. If you're late for the next scene, the Boss will be really mad."

The Boss smiled. "Is that so?"

"Yep." Mr. Roberts put his arm around me and we walked up the hill together.

CHAPTER
TWENTY-THREE

"If Mr. Roberts finds out we're not in our room getting ready for the banquet, we're going to be the main course instead of chicken," said Eugene.

"Come to think of it," I replied, "you might be better than the main course."

"Not enough meat to go around now," joked Wendy.

"As soon as we get these last two titles inserted," said Andi, "we'll put in the background music and be done."

"Shh," said Eugene. "What was that?"

Wendy looked out the window. "There's nothing there."

"That does it," said Andi. "Where's the tape recorder?"

"Shh. I just heard it again."

"Look, I'm going to open the door and settle this once and for all." I pushed the door open. "Satisfied? See there's—"

"What's going on in here?" said a voice from outside. We

froze. "What are the four of you doing in here now?" Nobody moved. "Aren't you supposed to be getting ready for the banquet?"

"Hi, Dan," I said weakly. "Can you keep a secret?"

The last of the dirty dishes were being bused from the tables when Mr. Roberts stood up at his place and banged on his water glass with a knife. While everyone got quiet Eugene and I slipped out, as if we were going to the bathroom.

"I hope everyone is having as good a time as I am tonight," we heard Mr. Roberts say from the other room. "*Simba* is the longest and most intricate video feature we've tried to date. If everything goes as planned, the premiere will be sometime in October." There was a resounding round of applause. "This year we are also going to enter *Simba* in an international film festival contest for high school and college films, and I think we're going to win it!" Mr. Roberts sat down amid another round of applause.

It was then I appeared from the back dressed in a trench coat and baseball cap. On the front of the coat hung a sign in big red letters that read THE BOSS. On the cap was a smaller sign that read I MAKE TROUBLE. I continued up to the front of the room, making sure to notice Mr. Roberts's expression when I went by. Whew, he was smiling.

"I'm waiting for your attention. We're all ready." I took a giant watch out of my pocket. "Let's see. The big hand's on the five and the little hand's on the . . . anyway, I know we're behind." The snickering was turning to laughter.

I took off the trench coat and underneath I was wearing one of the Boss's sport jackets. The sleeves were much longer than my arms and I had to push them up constantly. "Uhumm . . . uhumm. Can someone set up a video projector and screen for me?" While Wendy and Andi set up the screen and Eugene set up the projector, I carefully filled a red plastic bubble pipe with soap and blew bubbles. *"Ready? Lights! Projector! Roll 'em!"*

W E SQUARED PRODUCTIONS

in conjunction with

ANDI ENTERPRISES

PRESENT

THE BOSS??

The first scene showed me dressed as I was now, standing behind a table. "I guess you all are wondering why I called this special meeting tonight." The camera cut to Wendy and Eugene sleeping. "Tonight we open the Christmas-giving campaign. You'll notice a small tree at the back of the auditorium." On the screen was a picture of a giant redwood tree. "Eventually the tree is covered with—" Red, silver, and gold balls came flying at me from all directions and the scene faded.

The second scene opened with Andi standing beside a camera, looking perplexed. "Boss, Boss, I need help."

"What can I do for you?" I asked.

"This camera doesn't work."

"Let me take a look and see what's wrong." I looked into the camera for a few seconds, and as I said, "I don't see anything wrong," our camera zoomed in for a close-up of my face and I have a big black eye.

A collage of clips secretly taken by us followed.

"Aren't you ever going to get this right?" shouted Mr. Roberts.

"I did it just like you told me," I shouted back.

"No, Wendy, no!"

"Eugene! Will you ever wake up?"

"What kind of a camera angle is that, Andi? The audience will have to tilt their heads to see what's going on."

COME ON BABY LET'S DO THE
RAGING ROBERTS

A still of Mr. Roberts appeared. His arms were crossed and a scowl blackened his face. As the "Mexican Hat Dance" played he uncrossed his arms, waved them skyward, and looked toward the heavens. He turned around three times and threw his hat to the ground. Suddenly his hat flew back onto his head, he turned three times in the opposite direction, and refolded his arms. This was repeated three times. The audience cheered and clapped in time to the music.

The video ended with a series of stills:

Mr. Roberts hugging Eugene and Wendy.

Mr. Roberts giving Andi the thumbs-up sign.

Mr. Roberts, arms folded, smile on his face, watching a video monitor.

Mr. Roberts holding up ten fingers.

Mr. Roberts sitting in his director's chair, baseball cap pulled down over his eyes, sleeping.

All the kids surrounding Mr. Roberts clapping.

THANKS, BOSS
FROM ALL THE KIDS AT CINEKYD

As the lights went on Mr. Roberts stood up and applauded us. Inside I was applauding him.

TWENTY-FOUR

THE MAKING OF SIMBA

ACTUAL SHOOTING TIME	80 HOURS
LAYOUT OF CREDITS	24 HOURS
PRODUCTION OF SLIDES FOR CREDITS	6 HOURS
FILMING OF CREDITS	8 HOURS
CATALOGUING OF ALL VIDEOTAPE SHOT	21 HOURS
INITIAL PREPARATORY EDITING (FIRST DONE ON PAPER THEN ON VIDEOTAPE)	100 HOURS
ACTUAL VIDEOTAPE EDITING	150 HOURS
MUSICAL SCORING	20 HOURS
PREPARATION OF AUDIO SCRIPT (WRITING, NARRATION, TIMING TAPES, ETC.)	100 HOURS
FINAL SOUNDTRACKING	16 HOURS
TOTAL:	525 HOURS

WHEW!

PREMIERE   SATURDAY OCTOBER 15

I looked at the clock once more. Time was moving at a snail's pace. I leaned back in my chair and closed my eyes.

"Gene? Started your weekend already?"

What a sense of humor my English teacher has. "Huh, yeah . . . I guess so," I replied. Would last period ever end? It wasn't only the premiere that was on my mind. It was . . . no, it was too crazy. This only happens in the movies. It would be great, though. I smiled because I knew now I could pull it off.

Ring ring. School was finally over. I walked out of the room and headed down the hall to my locker. Halfway there I stopped. When I was sure no one was looking, I closed my eyes, gritted my teeth, and banged my fists against my thighs as I repeated silently, *Go get 'em, Simba. You can do it!* I took a long, deep breath, puffed out my chest, and headed down the hall in the opposite direction.

When I got to the familiar steel double doors of the wrestling room, I pushed them open and looked around until I saw Todd. He looked smaller than I remembered, but there was no mistaking, it was him.

Todd smiled when he recognized me. "I guess you didn't believe me," he said with a nasty laugh. "I told you next time it'll be for real."

I froze. Was I crazy? Was I signing my death warrant? When I reached the center of the mat, I motioned for Todd to join me.

"Either you've got more guts than I thought you had or you're just plain weird," said Todd as he approached me. Everything stopped as the wrestlers lined the sides of the mat to watch.

When we were almost touching, I jerked my head suddenly to the left. As Todd turned to look, I grabbed his right arm with such force that it spun him around. My heart was racing and I could feel every hair on my body standing up at attention. With a bloodcurdling yell, I wrapped my left arm around his waist and squeezed.

"If we were wrestling right now, you'd be looking at the cracks in the ceiling," I shouted. To Todd's surprise, I loosened my grip. "But I wouldn't do that to you in front of all these guys." Without any warning I tightened my grip again and yanked Todd backward. "The heck I wouldn't!"

Everyone roared, only this time it wasn't at me. I reached into my pocket and dropped two tickets onto Todd's chest. "Tomorrow night is the premiere of *Simba the Wildling* at Cinekyd. I hope to see you there." I started to walk off the mat, but when I got to the door, I stopped. "If not, I'll see you here Monday. What weight did you say you were trying out for?"

Half out of breath, I walked proudly down the hall toward my locker.

"Hi, Gene." It was Andi. "Are you okay?"

"Sure," I replied. "Why do you ask?"

"Your face is all red and your hair's messed up. Were you just in a fight?"

"Fight?" I said laughingly. "It was no contest." I took a minute to catch my breath. "Are you going to help out at the video workshop tomorrow morning?" She nodded. "And are you going to the premiere at night?" Another nod. "Eugene and Wendy and I were thinking of going out for pizza between the workshop and the premiere. Wanna come?"

Andi grabbed my hand. "Sure." This time I squeezed back.

During the second hour of the video workshop the large group was divided into four smaller ones and makeup was

141

passed out so that everyone could try putting it on. There were some great photographs to be had and I wasn't going to miss one. I quietly inched down toward one group, hoping to catch some candid shots. There, standing just outside the group and off to the side, was a small, skinny boy. It was difficult to see his expression since he was staring at the ground, but from what I did see I could tell he wasn't too happy.

I walked over to Mr. Roberts, who had already begun to take pictures of another group. "Can I borrow your camera?" I asked.

"Why do you need another one?"

"Do you see that boy down there?" Mr. Roberts nodded. "I think he wants to help me take pictures!"

Mr. Roberts handed me his camera. "Don't push him if he doesn't want to."

"Hey. Remember what you told me. This is my show now."